EMERSON WOLVES BOOK 1

KATHI S. BARTON

WCP

World Castle Publishing, LLC
Pensacola, Florida

Copyright © Kathi S. Barton 2014
Print ISBN: 9781629891286
eBook ISBN: 9781629891293
First Edition World Castle Publishing, LLC, July 25, 2014
http://www.worldcastlepublishing.com

Licensing Notes

Cover: Karen Fuller
Editor: Eric Johnston
Editor: Maxine Bringenberg

Prologue

Six year old Slone Morris knew better than to cry. It hurt too much when she was caught and it usually meant more pain when that happened...not from the tears, but from what her stepmother did to her when she caught her. But she had to pee, and she needed to stand up soon. Slone knew that the car ride had been a long one, and she was getting sore from not moving. Peeking out of the cage she was in, she tried to think of how to get Eva, her stepmother, to love her. Or at least like her just a little bit.

She had tried everything. Her room was always cleaned up and everything put away. It wasn't like there were a lot of toys to play with, and the ones she had were just to see, not to touch. Her books were in order from biggest to littlest like Eva liked them. She made her bed, too, as best she could, but it was never enough. Her daddy didn't hear her stories anymore either. No way. Boy, that had made Eva mad when she'd done that once. And she never called her "Mom" anymore either, at least when nobody was around but her and Eva. That was a bigger no-no than telling Daddy when he came back from his trips. No, Slone had done everything she could think of to make the scary woman like her enough to stop hurting her.

But this morning she'd really messed up, and she knew Eva was super-duper mad about it. Slone hadn't meant to drop the glass and spill the milk all over the kitchen like she had. It hadn't been her fault, but Eva hadn't wanted to listen to her. She never did.

Slone had tried to be quiet in the mornings like her stepmother wanted her to be. When Daddy wasn't home, Eva wanted to sleep until she woke up. And Slone knew that if she were ever caught in the kitchen or any other part of the house, she'd be put into the basement again for days and days. Plus, Slone was pretty sure she'd be beaten again if Eva found out she had a key to get out of the cage. But it had saved her from crying a couple of times when she'd been sure that Eva had forgotten about her for a couple of days.

The mailman had put a box on the stoop while she'd been in the kitchen, and Slone had put in on the table and not opened it, just like she'd been told to do a million times. But when she'd been pouring herself some milk, the box had beeped at her and she'd been scared. She didn't know if it was her screaming or the breaking glass that had woken Eva up.

Eva had come out of the bedroom toward Slone so fast she'd had no time to run. She'd hit her four times before Slone had been able to run to the pantry and shut the door. A lock had been put on the door several months ago, and Slone wished all the time that there was one on the other side, too. It would have made Eva mad, but maybe if she locked herself in there sometime, it would give Eva time to cool off or go to bed and forget her again. As it was, Eva had given her a good beating for running, then another one for screaming. Then she'd locked her in the pantry again.

Slone had laid there hurting for what seemed like forever before the door had been opened again. The light from the kitchen window made her jerk to cover her eyes, and the small moan was out before she could stop it.

"Shut up with your constant whining." Slone nodded and waited. She'd not been given permission to speak, and she didn't want to be hurt again. "Go to your room and get cleaned up. Put on those jeans you insist on wearing and one of those ridiculous tee-shirts. Hurry the fuck up, too."

Slone walked to her room and closed the door. It wouldn't do for her to get caught crying again, so she leaned against the door and cried quietly. After a few minutes, she went to her closet and pulled out pants and underwear. Her last tennis shoe was being tied when her door was opened and Eva stood there.

She was glad she'd already put her stash on her body before her shoes. Sometimes the little bags of food were all that kept her from begging for something to eat. And Slone now had them hidden all over the whole house, too. Standing up, she circled around when Eva told her to.

"You are the ugliest kid I've ever seen, you know that, right? I guess you'll have to do. Not that it'll matter after today what you wear." Eva left and Slone waited. It had been ground into her head and body not to do more until she was told. When Eva yelled come, Slone left her room, grabbing up the last piece of her stash from under her dresser. She had never had sweets that much and was hoping for some time today to get to eat it. A real candy bar. She ate it as soon as Eva got out of the car. It was better than she'd thought it would be.

The car door opened just as Slone was reaching for her little Baggie of crackers. The car was smelling up with hair spray, so Slone knew that Eva had gotten her hair done.

She nearly coughed but caught herself just in time. The smell was overwhelming.

They were moving again once the engine was started. The drive seemed to take forever. By the time they got to wherever Eva was taking them, Slone had to pee so badly it hurt. And when they finally stopped, she heard the door open almost immediately and wondered if they'd gone back home. When the back of the car opened and her stepmother was standing there, Slone was suddenly terrified. The look on her face was scarier than she'd ever seen it before.

"You'll do as you're told or so help me I'll make you regret ever being born. Why your mother left you everything is beyond me. But there's the thirty-four million dollar question, now isn't it?" Slone had no idea what she was talking about but nodded. "Well, I've had enough of the both of you. Him for lying to me all these years, and you for...well, for being you. I cannot stand another moment with you around."

The door closed again, and she was plunged into darkness. The animal cage she rode in when her daddy wasn't around was covered on the top, and she couldn't see much. And what little she could see didn't help her. She was tossed around again as the car moved. The jerking movement was too much, and she did something she knew was going to get her into big trouble. Slone wet her pants.

Crying quietly, Slone thought of what would happen to her when she got home. The things that Eva would do to her would be horrible. No dinner for sure and no breakfast either, she'd bet. And she'd have to wear her pants to school for a week, too. Slone was still crying when the car stopped again.

"Oh hello." It took Slone a few seconds to realize that it was Eva speaking. Her voice was soft and sweet like when she talked to people on the phone. Never how she spoke to her or her daddy sometimes. "Yes, I've been having a *me* day. Little Slone is at the sitters on some outing, so I went to the mall and had my hair done, too. I was trying to find her something for her birthday. You know how little girls are and their parties."

As she told the person on the phone about the party, Slone thought about it as well. She didn't want a party. She never had any fun, so worried about her dress getting dirty or one of the guests saying the wrong thing to her stepmother. And the presents were all donated to some charity even before she was able to see them. Then she had to write thank-you notes to the guests as if she had played with and loved them very much. Slone hated her birthday. The car door suddenly opened, and she cringed away from it.

Eva stared at her for a long time before she spoke. "You've pissed your pants? You actually pissed your fucking pants?" Her voice got higher with each word. "Mother fuck. Now I'll have to scrub the carpet in here. Get out." It was too much, and Slone broke one of the hard rules that she knew was going to hurt her badly. She begged.

"No, please. Don't hurt me. I'll be good. I promise I will. I'll scrub the car. Please don't hurt me." Cringing away from her as far as she could in her confined space, Slone tried to curl into a tiny ball. But she was jerked from the cage and thrown to the ground. Her head exploded in pain when she hit the car bumper. Then Eva kicked her several times as she held her down with her hand on her head. Slone threw up twice, but nothing but bile came out.

When she was jerked up and dragged along without another word, Slone cried. Not even when she fell twice did Eva stop dragging her along behind her by her hair. Begging did no good; not even screaming at her stopped the woman from wherever she was taking her. Slone just knew it was going to be somewhere dark and she'd never be let out. It wasn't until they stopped that Slone looked around.

The water beside them was running really fast. The rocks in the water just peeked above the surface in places, and the giant stone they were standing on was damp with water as it sprayed up over it. Slone looked at Eva.

"Get in." Slone started to back away. "You heard me, get in the water. I'm sick to death of you and your shit, and I'm disposing of you right now."

"I can't swim." Eva shrugged and laughed. "I'll drown. You said I was never to go near the water. I can't get in there. I won't see my daddy again."

"I got news for you. You aren't going to anyway. I took care of that little problem yesterday morning. So distraught over your drowning, he crawled into his car and let the running engine take all his woes away." Slone shook her head. "Oh yes. And when your body is found downstream in a few days, if ever, I will be one wealthy widow."

When she lunged at her, Slone fell. Her entire body hit the water so hard that it took her breath away. Then the cold took away her ability to breathe at all. Slone new she was going to die. She was holding on to the branch near the stone she'd been standing on when she saw a black flash of something hit her stepmother.

~~~

Willie had been following the two of them for the past ten minutes. He had wanted to intervene on the child's part, but had two things going against him. First of all, and most likely the most important of all reasons, he was currently a big wolf. That would have made it hard to make anyone see reason, if he thought he could have reasoned with the woman. The second, even if he had shifted to his human self, his clothes were all the way across the park in his car. He just hated that the little girl was suffering so much at the woman's hands.

Willie loved children, everyone knew that. He had a son and a daughter-in-law that he loved more than anything in the world. His son was a little on the whiney side most of the time, and his wife the same, but they were gonna, in a few months, make him a grandda. His wife, God rest her soul, would have been in seventh heaven with that. But this woman was treating this child like an animal. Hell, worse than an animal.

He could hear her talking to her. Yelling more like it. Telling her that she was worthless and other such horrible things. There was no way he was going to leave her because he had a feeling that whatever this human bitch had planned for the child, it was not going to end well. He'd even mentally reached for his son, the cop over in their little burg.

I got me a license plate I need you to see to. I'm out here on the back part of our land and there's something going on here that I might need you to help me with. His son said he'd run it and get back with him. Then the woman hit the little girl and she took a tumble into the water. Willie reacted before he thought better of it.

He hit the woman first. He was afraid that if he didn't get her out of the way, she'd hurt them both before he could save the child. As soon as she went head-over-ass into the water, he reached for the child. She was barely hanging on, and her head was bobbing up and down in the water like a bobber on a fishing line. He grabbed her tiny wrist into his mouth.

The snapping bones sounded like a gun going off in his head. But it was the scream that had him holding on. If he let her go now, she'd never survive. And if he shifted to help her, he'd lose her for sure. Pulling her as hard as he could, he got her head on the stone just as he realized that her shirt was caught on the limb. The current was tugging her back two inches for every one he pulled her up. She was nearly underwater again when he reached out his paw and dug it into her small thigh.

He was glad that by then she was unconscious. Willie knew that he was hurting her, and he hated it. His own heart, old and bruised from the accident, started to pain him a little more than he wanted as well. His son reached for him when he realized he was going to lose the child and himself if he didn't do something now.

That car, a big, black SUV? It belongs to a man by the name of Truman Morris. Not reported missing or stolen. Why you asking? You didn't hit his car, did you? Damn it, Dad, you should have called me if you wanted to go out. He couldn't answer his son, trying to think what to do. *Dad? Are you all right?"*

I didn't hurt nobody, and I told you before that I can drive as well as you. She's tried to kill her. You have to...come to the old quarry where the river runs the fastest. There's an old granite stone there that we fish off of, remember? His son said yes and asked him what was wrong. *I'm not going to make it. But the child must. She's...she's had it hard and you have to promise me that you'll save her.*

Dad, please just come here. I'll see to you. Or wait there. I'll come to you and get you help. Is it your heart again? Dad? Tell me. Whatever you're up to, I want you to stop it right now and get home. I don't know what this kid has to do with anything, but I can't take her. I don't want a child right now, hardly the one I got coming. Do you know what it's going to do to my life? Willie could feel his tears as he held the child, knowing that he was leaving her better off but not by much. Her head was back in the water and if he didn't do something soon, they'd both be dead.

Find her for me. Promise me. I want you to – The current nearly took her, and he had to scramble to keep her. Sinking his claws into her leg, Willie felt her bones break there as well. Taking his mouth from her wrist, he reached for her leg and was going to pull her out that way, but the current shifted her again and he sank his fangs into her soft belly. She was as good as dead if he left her now. *I'm having to change her. If I don't, she's going to be dead when you get here. Her mother…the woman in the car with her… tried to kill her. I did the only thing I could do and hit her with my body to knock her away.*

Dad, I'm coming. I'll be there – He cut his son off. He knew there was no way he was going to live through this, and he needed to tell him what had happened.

Hush and listen to me. Find the child and if she can be saved, I want you to tell her that I'm sorry I had to do it. I didn't want her to die. He sank his teeth deeper into her belly and pulled her completely out of the water and onto the stone. Willie held her in his mouth, hoping that she wasn't too weak to take the conversion. *She's going to need someone to care for her, teach her about what I've done to her.*

You're converting her. It wasn't a question, but he answered his son when he sounded pissed anyway. *Dad, there are laws. Just let her go. Please. Keep yourself safe and let her go.*

I can't. I should have helped her sooner and now she just might die anyway. Poor child. The woman had her caged in the back of that big car like someone would do a dog. She was dragging her around by her hair like she were less than human. I couldn't have left her to die like she planned, and neither would you have.

The pain got to be too much and he had to leave her. Closing the connection to his son, he told him he loved him very much and pulled his teeth free of the child. As soon as he did, she screamed again and again. Willie watched her for several seconds to make sure she wasn't going to roll into the water again and moved away. He had to get away from her.

If they found him lying beside her, he knew it would shame his family and the child. A grown naked man with a small dead child would be all they could see. His son would know the truth of it, of course, but he'd not be able to say a word. No, Willie thought, his best bet was to get as far from her as he could and hope that she lived.

His heart was beating so hard in his chest that he had to look twice to see if it was pounding right out of him. Willie was dizzy, too. His vision was fading in and out, and he had to stop more often than he'd hoped to rest before he could move again.

The sirens were sounding in the distance when he finally had to lay down. There was no way he could stay where he was if he could hear them that well, so he started to stand again. But all he managed to do was fall over, and he knew it was the end. Lying there, he looked up at the bright sun and thought of his life.

William, his son, had been such a joy to him after his missus had passed. He'd been a whiney boy and had gone from a spoiled child to a worse adult. Willie knew it was his fault, but he'd been so lonely. He was going to miss him most. And then there was his grandbaby.

"I wish I could have met you, little man." Willie smiled as his body began to shut down. He could no longer lift his arm, and his legs were just lumps of meat and bones. But he'd do it all again if he had to. "The little girl needed me."

"Well, of course, she did." He opened his eyes, just realizing that he'd closed them, and looked at his lovely wife. "You ready to come to me? You old poop, you should have taken that little bag that William got you with some clothes in it. You might have lived a little longer had you done it."

"I know, but I wasn't planning on meeting up with a mad woman." He closed his eyes when the pain in his chest seemed to triple in an effort to end him. "Did you see the child, my love? Did you see those eyes? Aged beyond her years, I think. And such sadness."

"The woman is dead. Saw her myself. Her body, a broken mess down there at the bottom of our ravine. I don't think they'll be opening her casket up for viewing unless they have some miracle stuff down in them hollows." Willie nodded. "You need to come along now. William and the others are looking for you."

He sat up for her and felt...he turned to look at the shell he'd been in. He looked good, he thought, and his Meggie smacked him. He winked at her as he moved along the field back to where the child and his son were.

"She'll make it. You converted her, but it will be a long road for her before it kicks in all the way. You almost didn't get her to the other side." Willie nodded. "You did well. She'll live to fight another day."

"I hope so." The medics worked at her little body as he watched them. He'd broken her arm and her leg by pulling her out of the water, and the claw marks on her little bottom were nasty. "Never meant to hurt her that badly, but she was falling in and I had to save her."

"She'll live is what you should be thinking, not how you had to do it. And William and the others, they're looking for you, too." William had sent two of his men, both of them pack, to find him. He'd told them to find him and to stay with him until this was finished. He'd even handed one of them one of the small bags that held clothes.

"They're gonna dress me so that I ain't nekked when they find me?" He felt his pride for his son go up a few notches. "I'm going to miss him a great deal."

"I do as well. And his wife, Jess. Do you think they'll ever grow up? I despair of it, if you want to know the truth of it. We did some terrible things when he was a baby by not making him mind like we should have. But there isn't anything we can do about that now. I just hope he watches over the child some." Willie nodded as they loaded the young child into the back of the awaiting ambulance. She was going to make it was all he could think about.

"Are you ready?" He looked at Meggie and knew a kind of love for her that others would only hope to attain. He pulled her into his arms, having missed the way she fit against his body. "You old poop. How I've missed you, too."

"We have to see to her. Just for a bit longer." He felt her nod. "I've never worked so hard to save a person before, wolf or human. She's…oh Meggie, you should have seen her fight. Wanted out of that water like it was her business. And she was…that woman deserves nothing of her. I'm glad she's dead."

"Me, too. I never seen it happen, but I know you to tell the truth. Poor child." He opened his eyes and found himself standing next to the child again. She was in surgery now and they were working hard to put her back together. The tubes running in and out of her were making a right racket, but he watched her closely.

Leaning down to her ear, he felt the connection to her. It wasn't strong like it might have been had he lived, but it was there. "You'll live. Don't make my gift to you be for nothing, child. Live and find someone to love you, as I do my own Meggie. You'll find him someday and when you do, you'll be so happy that you didn't drown in that water."

They watched her for a few minutes longer, but Willie felt the pull of something. He looked at Meggie when she smiled at him. It was time, well past time for them to go. Looking at the little girl again, her body was so abused he felt tears for her suffering, and he told her again to live. As he faded out, he heard the machines in the room start to scream, and he felt his heart weigh just a bit heavier. She didn't make it, he just knew it. The poor, poor child, didn't make it.

Chapter 1

Twenty-two years later in Sommersville, Ohio.

"You've no idea how glad I am that you've decided to take this off my hands." Hunter Emerson just looked at his brothers and said nothing as the man across from them continued. They were there for support, but all he wanted to do was take his aching head home and crawl into bed. The eight of them had partied too much last night for this early of a meeting. Then Pete Skills spoke again, and he turned back to ask him what he'd said.

"I said this is a good group you're starting out with. Some of the pack is a mite on the older side, but not many. Most of them are about you and your brothers' age. But settled, too. I think that only one or two of them are job-seeking right now, what with the plant shutting down. Then there's Miss Giles. She ain't no trouble, mind you, but you might want to stay on her good side."

"Why is that?" Hunter looked at Luke, who had done the research on this pack when the advertisement for them looking for a new Alpha had come across his desk. He'd done a great deal of background checks on all the members, and he'd never heard of a Giles woman. "I didn't see her name on the rosters."

"She won't be either. And so you know, we ain't seen hide nor hair of her since…well, I ain't never seen her to be honest. Miss Giles was holed up in that place when I took over about ten years ago. She keeps to herself and never bothers any of us. She does support us when we need it, but we don't bother her none. It was written in the contract that we was to never seek her out and she'd do her part of it without any problems. She owns all the pack land and even most of the buildings here and in town. All of them successful, too."

He looked at Luke again, who handed him a copy of the contract that he'd been meaning to read over. He glanced at it and read the parts that had little tabs next to them. It was there…a person by the name of Slone M. Giles owned all four hundred acres that the pack used, as well as the land that the pack-house and other out buildings were on. There was an additional two thousand that was supposedly off-limits to everyone.

"When do we meet this woman? I'm assuming she comes to the pack meetings and will be at the one where you introduce me, right?" Pete was already shaking his head. "Why is that?"

"She don't want any of us to bother her." Hunter started to speak, but Pete held up his hand. "Yeah, before you ask, she is a wolf. Not a pureblood, I'm to understand, but one made. She don't want a damned thing to do with any of us and since she don't charge us any rent and pays for all the upkeep on the buildings, we all just let her have her way."

Hunter nodded to his brother, Jarrett. He'd find out what he could about the woman and see what sort of things she was doing all holed up like Pete had said. He also wanted to find out what kind of deal she was giving them on the taxes and upkeep. Surely she was taking a big chunk of the pack monies, too.

They worked through the morning and well into the afternoon getting all the things settled. Jarrett had left at eleven and then the rest just after lunch. They each had their assignment to take care of, but it was Luke he wanted to talk to most. When he came out of the pack house, Luke was leaning against his car talking to a pretty, young woman.

"This is Rachel. She was just telling me what sort of pack meetings they had." Hunter nodded at the woman, wishing her away. But Luke had something to tell him and he was using this girl to do it. "Did you know that they have very liberal thinking when it comes to sex? I mean, there is no law that says they have to protect their females."

Hunter looked at the girl who was popping gum and smiling at him like he was Thanksgiving turkey all tussled up for her. He shivered when he thought of what else this girl had to tell them.

"What sort of pack doesn't protect its females?" She grinned bigger, and he wanted to step back.

"We protect the little ones and the ones that want to save themselves for marrying." She made it sound that that was the last thing on her mind. "But we older ones, we can pretty much do what we want, when we want, to whoever we want."

She looked all of twenty, if that, and he doubted that she'd seen too much in the way of school either. To prove her point about being free, she leaned into Luke, who looked at him over the woman's head. She ran her hands down his brother's chest to his cock and cupped him. Luke pushed her away with a slight grimace.

"You don't have to worry none about me telling on you. There's a bunch of us that have all sorts of fun when it comes to the Alpha. Not old Pete, but the others that come in thinking about taking over. We can work you over really well for a price." Luke looked at him, and Hunter could see that he wasn't happy as the girl continued. "We're using the money to fund us a trip to Hollywood where we can get into the pictures."

Hunter had no doubt as to what sort of movies this woman had in mind. When she reached for him, he backed up several steps and nearly fell over Pete, who had come up behind him. He looked at the girl when she dropped to her knees.

"What did I tell you about coming around here? It was told to you and the other women that you're not a member of this pack and you're to stay off pack land." She nodded, then stood up. The gun was in her hand before any of them could react to it. "What the Sam Hill do you think you're doing?"

The gun went off just as Pete smacked it out of her hand. It went flying, and it wasn't until he dropped to the ground that Hunter realized he'd been hit. The pain in his chest made him dizzy, and he looked down at the spreading blood. Luke was screaming at him just as he watched Pete snap the girl's neck and drop her.

"Shift, you motherfucker, before you die." Hunter heard the words but couldn't make them work in his fuzzy head. The slap got his attention. "Shift, Hunter, before you bleed to death."

His wolf took him. The pain of the bullet shifted out of his body when his human disappeared. As his wolf, he laid there for several minutes while Luke spoke on the phone. It wasn't until he could stand that Luke spoke to him again.

"You'll have to leave here now. The police are on their way and if you're about, they'll wonder what the hell happened." The gun went off again, and they looked at Pete as he fell backwards. He dropped the gun just as the blood started to pour from his shoulder. "It was his idea. We have a story ready for them, but you have to be gone."

He's taking the fall? Hunter didn't want that to happen. He'd been shot and now the older man was bleeding. *No, I can't let that happen.*

The sirens were sounding in the distance, and Hunter backed from his brother when he kicked out at him. He was terrified of being caught like a wolf, but didn't want Pete to go to jail.

"They had a public fight the other day, and she threatened him. Nothing is going to happen. Will you please get your ass out of here? I have to clear out your prints yet." Hunter looked down and then at Luke. "It was his idea. Go."

He left but not before turning back to see his brother kicking dust up. There would be almost nothing of him being there to show, and what was there could be explained. Going to just the edge of the forest behind the pack house, he watched as three cruisers and an ambulance pulled up. He disappeared into the woods when it looked like old Pete wasn't going to be arrested.

When he circled around the woods to the hotel they were staying in, he saw his brother, Ellis, standing next to his truck. He tossed a bag in his general direction, and Hunter picked it up with his teeth and took it to the back of the building to change. When he came back around, both Ellis and Jarrett were standing there.

"There is less on this Giles woman than I like. I mean, she does own about all the town, but not because she bought it. The town was built on her land, and she simply gets rent in return for their use, just the town proper. The pack pays nothing, and she seems to be the one who cares for it all, too. Again, just the pack. The town does for themselves, but she has to approve it. The bank in town has no record of her having money in it, so I've stretched out my search to see what else I can find. And before you ask me, yes, I did see if she is taking pack funds. She's not." Hunter waited for the rest, knowing there had to be more. But Jarrett just stood there.

"You do know that this woman is a wolf that owns us lock, stock, and barrel, right? And she can shove us off her land at a whim." Jarrett shook his head. "What's that supposed to mean?"

"No, she can't. The contract that I've tried to get you to read for the past two weeks states that we have as much right to the land as she does. And so long as she's not bothered by any members of the pack or anyone else, we can simply live there on her land. It's a win-win for both of us." Hunter knew there was more to this than that and wanted to meet this woman now more than ever. "Don't do it, Hunter. Leave it alone."

"She can't be all that generous. No one is. How long has she been caring for the pack? How much is she getting in return, and what is she doing with all her privacy? Selling drugs? Growing them? For all we know, she's got the biggest meth lab in the country out there and we can go down when she does."

"You're just grasping at straws. You and I both know this is just going to get us into trouble if you don't back off." Hunter felt his temper rise, and Ellis stepped in front of him.

"Back off, big brother. This is no reason for us to shed blood." He watched Jarrett as he moved into the hotel. "Come on, let's go and see what we can find out before we piss this woman off. She's probably this old broad that had grayed out so badly that you can't see her in the snow. And she has like five million cats."

"Cats don't like us." Hunter shook his body and calmed his wolf while his brother stood in front of him. "I didn't even want to do this. You guys did. And it wasn't until this morning that you told me I'd be the Alpha. We're all alphas. Why me?"

"You're the oldest, and Dad said so." Hunter looked around for their father, suddenly not so happy he might be there. "He's still back home seeing to the move. You should also know that he is expecting us to have a cook hired and a staff in place when he gets here next week. He's not going to be too thrilled with you if you get us kicked off the land before he gets here."

"He'd want answers, too." Ellis nodded but said nothing more. "I'm fine now, you can back the fuck off."

Ellis leaned against the truck again. "I heard about the girl. Christ, on your first day you had to kill someone."

"Pete did it. Then shot himself so I could get away. I don't know what would have happened if I had stayed around, but I'm pretty sure they would have shot my ass full of holes, then asked questions. People don't take well to large wolves in their area." Ellis laughed, as did Hunter. "She was going to shoot us."

"I heard. You okay?" Hunter nodded. "Good. We have a problem other than the two women. The house that we're supposed to live in isn't fit for us. Not fit for anybody as a matter of fact. I've called Dad and he's sending some of the crew out ahead of him to get the thing up to code. In the meantime, I've made arrangements to stay here until we can find a house to rent."

They were getting in the truck to have a look at the house when Jarrett came toward them. Lee and Graham, two more brothers, were right behind him. It seemed that the gang was all there with the exception of Luke. And he was going to meet them at the house. The Emerson men were back in business, it seemed.

~~~

Slone read the email twice, then shut down her computer. So there was a new Alpha in town. She moved to the kitchen where she had some things simmering on the stove and looked out the window. It always made her nervous when new people moved into town.

The house and the property around it were secure. She'd had the electric fence put in almost as soon as she'd bought the place. And the six strands of barbed wire made it almost impossible to get to her. She knew that most people would give her what she wanted, but there were others out there that would have to have just a little more. So far, she'd not had a bit of trouble. But new always meant someone might want more answers. And she wasn't willing to share.

William and Jess Giles had shielded her from most of the questions when she'd been a child. Most of what had happened that day she hadn't found out until later. Her stepmother had not just tried to kill her, but had killed her father as well. And her body, broken and almost unrecognizable, was found a few weeks later in the large pool of water down from the falls where she'd gone over. It seemed that Eva got what she deserved.

In all the time since, Slone had never told anyone about the wolf who had saved her and the fact that he was the one that had knocked Eva over into the fast-moving water. The only person who had known anything was William, and only, he told her, because his father had told him before he'd died. Slone turned to the computer when it made a sound indicating that she had mail.

"Urgent," the note said. Smiling, she opened the email from Pete and wondered what he considered urgent now. As soon as she read the first line, she began to worry more. The letter told her of the death of one of the wolves, as well as about the new Alpha that the newsletter hadn't mentioned. He also told her that the house was unfit for the new Alpha. The company from town had done a half-assed job for them again.

"I don't think this new Alpha, Hunter Emerson, is going to honor your privacy, Miss Giles. In fact, if he doesn't try and contact you soon, it will be something of an oddity to me. He's bound and determined to meet you." Slone thought that he could try, but she was a good deal more experienced in hiding than the average person and could hold out longer than he could. She never had to leave here if she didn't want to. "I have given him your email address before hand with the contract, so he will be contacting you soon that away. If he don't, then good, but I don't think he's going to be that way. He and his five brothers seem to have their heads on straight and will do a good job for the pack, much better than I did."

She thought about what to say back to the man. She'd never met him, of course, and he could, for all she knew, be as bad as the other Alphas she'd met in her lifetime. But she hadn't been bothered, and that was what she genuinely wanted.

"Alpha. I thank you for the information. Please continue to discourage Mr. Emerson from contacting me person to person. He can email me all he wishes and I will answer each of them until the point where he becomes annoying. I have been very generous with my efforts to keep the pack together, but I will not hesitate to pull back anything and everything if he pushes this too far.

"As for the house. I will take care of it in the morning. You will see an improvement on it as soon as noon. Please advise the new Alpha that things will be set to right soon."

She signed her name at the bottom and hit send. Almost as soon as it said "view message" she received another email, this one from a person with the handle name of lemerson. Slone assumed it was from the Alpha, but it wasn't; it was from his brother.

Miss Giles. My name is Luke Emerson and I am the attorney for the new pack, as well as for my family. I wanted to take this time to introduce myself, as I will be the one dealing with all correspondence from now on. As I have mentioned, I am an attorney and one of good standing.

I'm very sorry to hear that you'll not be meeting with us at the next pack meeting. We will be introducing the new Alpha and all of us, his brothers. Perhaps it would be a good time now to set up a time for us to meet with you to go over some of our expectations. You, no doubt, have a few questions of your own to ask us. As attorney for the pack, I, too, have some questions about what is in the contract with you and the pack.

Additionally, we wanted to see what sort of provisions you have made for the pack in concerns of the land and taxes. It is our understanding that you pay those, but we cannot find where you are being reimbursed in any way from the pack. I have pointed out that it is my job to make sure that things are on the up and up, and it is my duty to make sure that nothing untoward is going on. My brother, Hunter, wants to make a new start and wants to bring you in on the startup.

He signed it with his name and title.

She went to the kitchen to cool off before she replied.

After she had a nice dinner of stew, she sat down at the computer again to see if she could work out an answer that didn't light a fire under the attorney's ass. Slone didn't want to start off on the wrong foot with these new pack members, but she also didn't want them to think she was a pushover. She'd been that enough.

Attorney Emerson. I am using your title, as you seem to be exceptionally proud of it. I, however, don't care at all if you are an attorney or a surgeon. I simply want to be left alone.

There are no taxes that you have to worry about, as I own the land. There also is no reason for you to worry about reimbursements; as I have said, I own the buildings on the land. As for a meeting…well, that's simply not going to happen.

I cherish my privacy, as I'm sure you do as well. I mean, you would hate very much for it to get out that you were caught with your pants down around your ankles during hazing week your senior year. Also, it would not look well for the youngest Emerson if word got around that during high school his girlfriend told her parents that she'd been raped by him. I know that she later recanted her story, but it will not go away if you pursue wanting to meet me. And yes, I've had you all investigated.

Now, as I was saying, I own the land, the buildings, and about everything else in this little town. I ask for nothing in return, I don't expect any sort of reimbursement, and I never bother any of the Alphas. I do expect them, however, to leave me alone.

You may, at any time, email me. And I will answer as promptly as I can. There is no phone that I employ here in my part of my little world, so there is no way for you to call, so if you look for that option, you will be sorely disappointed. And mail, when I get it, is through channels that do not include the post office.

Enjoy your life in Sommersville, and I will enjoy my peace and quiet as well. Thank you.

Slone didn't bother putting her name on the email because she was pretty sure he could figure it out. Shutting down the computer completely this time, she went to her office and looked over the thing her own attorney had sent her that morning. It was nearly midnight when she went to bed.

She sat down on her bed and wondered if she'd ever feel like she could go into a room and close the door behind her. The entire house on each floor was devoid of doors between the rooms, and the windows at the back of the house were large and with no curtains at any of them. The view was spectacular, in that each window looked out over the river behind her house. The same river, in fact, that she'd nearly been killed in all those years ago just further upstream, and a good deal of distance from where she'd lived as a child. She lay down and wondered what the new Alpha would think about her if he knew just who was locked behind the large gates at her entrance.

"He'd want to shun me into leaving, and then where would he be?" Slone rolled to her side and looked out the darkened window. "Or he'd sell my whereabouts to the papers. Even after all this time, they still wonder about the girl who had been mauled by a wolf."

There were only scars on her body now to tell what might have happened to her back then. After she'd woken up in the hospital two weeks after her father's funeral, she'd taken a little longer to heal, but she'd eventually been able to get around all right. The move into the house with the Giles had been hard, but she'd made the best of it. It took her many years to get over waiting for Jess to hit her and to lock her away. They hadn't wanted her so she'd tried her best to be invisible to them as much as possible.

The Giles, William, and Jess, had taken her away that night and welcomed her into their family. It wasn't until a year later that she'd been told that the big wolf that had saved her life and changed it was also the big man's father. Being a wolf...a shifter, they'd said...had kept her from dying that day at the water. It had also changed her life in ways that no one outside the family knew about. There would be rumors then if she even hinted that she was a wolf.

"There are days when I wish you'd left me to drown." Closing her eyes, she willed her wolf forward and leapt from the bed. She was out of the house and into the wooded area behind it before she could think that she should be sleeping instead. She needed to run.

Her body was much bigger than the other wolves on the property. They had been here when she'd bought the house, and she saw no reason to run them off. They knew that she was different, she supposed, and most of them gave her a wide berth, but other than that, they seemed to coincide with one another well enough. She did have a good relationship, she supposed you could call it, with one of them. He was, for all intents and purposes, the Alpha of his pack. And he never bothered her either.

She ran until she was exhausted, then returned to her bedroom. Naked, she laid down and let sleep take her. Slone knew that she'd be awake in a few hours and would need to work in the garden. But for now, she slept.

Chapter 2

Hunter was pissed, and he knew when he was pissed he tended to act slightly irrationally. And right now he was as irrational as he'd ever been. This woman daring to threaten his family and thinking he was going to let her was more than he could take. He drove up to the gates and looked at the impressive "stay the fuck out" fence that surround the house.

"Mother fuck, she wasn't kidding when she said leave her alone. Do you suppose she has snipers with guns waiting for hapless men like you to try and break in?" Hunter glared at Luke when he spoke. "You have to admit, she is right about her privacy."

"I don't have to admit shit. I'm the Alpha here." Luke laughed and that just pissed him off more. "You won't think it's so funny when she has some idiot print the half truths about what really happened to you at the fraternity."

"Actually, I don't have a clue why, but I don't think she'll do it. You made me write that email and I told you all it was going to do was get her dander up. I don't think what she wrote back was anything less than I'd threatened her with. Only hers was more to the point while mine was a little more veiled." Luke sat on the hood of his car and looked at the gate while he continued. "Why do you want this so badly? None of us care."

"Because I don't like to be told no." He hated to admit that, and Luke only nodded instead of telling him how stupid that sounded. "She is a part of this pack or she's not. I'm the one running this thing, not her."

"Yeah, you're doing so well so far. You've managed to piss her off in less time than it did for us to move here, had the new landlord pissed off because you demanded that he let us take over his entire house and not just the upstairs, and let me see....oh yeah, Dad is on his way here because he thinks you've gone off the deep end. I'm thinking he might be right."

"Fuck off." Luke laughed, and Hunter stretched his neck muscles. He hated when Luke was right and knew that as soon as Dad got there, he was going to smack him in the back of the head. He had been a little over the top with the email, but now this was war. This old woman was going to know that Hunter Emerson meant business. He just had to figure out how to get to her now.

"How old do you suppose she is?" Luke didn't answer him, but he didn't care. "I'm thinking Dad's age. I don't know why, but she's amassed a great deal of money if she could afford to put in a fortress like this one."

"Maybe she inherited it and she's as rich as she wants to be." That didn't explain why she was like a hermit, and Hunter told Luke that. "Why does it matter? Maybe she was in a horrific accident and sued the company that was responsible and wants to keep others from seeing how disfigured she is. And here we are bothering her. Are you this dense when it comes to all business sense? I wouldn't think so, but you are pretty stupid about this."

"Why the hell are you even here?" He turned on Luke when a way of getting into the compound was not coming to him. "I mean, I said I'd rather go alone, and here you are. Maybe I wanted my privacy, too."

"You have five brothers living in the same house with you. Privacy doesn't even come into the picture." Hunter growled. "If you want to talk about something important, I have a list of them for you. Did you know that the bank in town is run by humans, and that they won't lend any money to the people they consider undesirables?"

"Who are they talking about?" Luke pointed at him, then himself. "That's the most ridiculous thing I've ever heard. How do they even know who we are?"

"There's a list. I tried to find out who started this thing, but all I got was that it was mandatory." Hunter looked at the gates, and Luke laughed. "You can't blame everything on her. And I doubt if she had a thing to do with it. It was just put in place a few years ago. And since then, she's been taking applications for loans to help out."

"No doubt charging an overinflated amount of interest, too." Luke sighed heavily and shook his head. "Don't tell me she doesn't charge them anything."

"Oh she does, but it's under prime and they have their lifetime to pay it back. So long as the people make some sort of payment a month and can prove that they're trying. She has a large following in town, so I'd be careful who I piss off about her there. They might tar and feather you. And the way you've been snapping at everyone, I'm pretty sure any one of us would help out." Hunter felt himself hate the woman more instead of less. "Why are you so hyped up to make this woman out to be a bad guy? I mean, shit, Hunter, she's making your life a great deal better and you haven't even met her."

"I'm going to find out what the hell she's up to." He moved to his car when his brother told him he had an email. There was an attachment. As soon as it opened, he watched himself leaning against the car, and his brother looking at the laptop. She was recording them. Luke even waved in the direction the stream seemed to be coming from. The next email was her telling them to move on please...the wolves, the wild ones, were nervous with them there.

"At least she didn't call the cops on us." They got back in the car and this time Luke drove. Hunter held onto the laptop and tried to think how to reason with the woman. He had no idea. Most women he met would have done anything for him, including anything sexual he wanted. He wasn't sure what to do with one that simply turned her back on him. He decided that he'd try emailing her and then let her deal with that. But he'd be tactful...just not nice, too.

Miss Giles. I think we got off on the wrong foot. I'd like to make amends if you'd let me. I've been slightly overbearing and pushing in my pursuit to understand why a woman such as yourself would do all this for a pack that she has no desire to be a part of. He read it to Luke as he drove them home. Luke told him three times to let it go. "I can't."

He was nearly finished with the email by the time they got to where they were staying, and sat in the car while he signed his name to it. He sent it on its way before he changed his mind. And he while he was watching the connect work, Hunter knew that he should have let Luke read it over. Hopefully she'd see that he was trying here and meet him halfway.

They were at dinner at the local diner when Luke told him that she'd responded. Hunter was almost excited because he knew that she had finally come to her senses and was going to see him. He didn't care if she saw the rest of his family, but he was Alpha here, and that was the least he could hope for. He should have known that things were not what he'd hoped for when Luke was laughing when he handed him the computer.

Mr. Emerson. Are you dense? Do you have a brain ailment that makes it impossible for you to understand some words? Perhaps you should ask your brothers to take you to the library. I hear there is a thick dictionary there. Doubtful that it is nearly as thick as your head seems to be, but I could be wrong about that.

There. Is. No. Way. I. Want. To. Meet. With. You. I broke it down in individual words so you could look it up better this way. I could have told you what they mean, but I don't have time to try and teach you rudimentary English and still get my work done as well. I think that you should stop emailing me unless it is something important, and to my way of thinking, meeting with you is not on that list. Please leave me alone, stop standing outside my home, and for the love of it all, would you please simply fuck the hell off? I will take actions you'll not like if you continue harassing me this way. I've reached the end of my patience with you.

Hunter wanted to throw the computer. But he simply laid it on the table and sat there for a long while. It wasn't until someone hit him in the back of the head that he looked up. His father sat across from him.

"What are you doing?" Hunter sat up straighter in his chair and tried to think what his dad might be talking about. "You pestering this girl to the point that she kicks this entire pack off the land because you got your panties in a twist? Is that the plan? Because if you ask me, it sucks."

"She's shut up in there and won't let anyone see her." Sounded lame even to him and his father just shook his head. "What if she's doing something that's going to get us into trouble? For all we know she could be the biggest drug lord in the world."

"That she could be. But she might also be a woman who wants you to leave her alone. Ever think of that? Or are you all pissy because she didn't leap into bed with you like every other female you meet?" Hunter flushed. He hated talking about sex with his father. Especially when he was pretty sure his dad was getting more than he was. "Tell me what you want and I'll have a talk with her myself."

"*You* can't get in to see her if she won't let *me*." His father simply leaned back in the chair. His dad would get in and speak to her even if for no other reason than to rub his nose in it. "I want to know what she's doing behind those gates. Where does all her money come from, and why does she not charge the pack any money to live here?"

"That's all?" His father made it sound so easy, but Hunter wasn't fooled. He knew that his dad was going to get answers or he'd know the reason why. "And if I get these answers for you, you'll let the woman go? You'll stop pissing in her oatmeal?"

"Yes, sir." His dad sat there for a bit longer, then nodded. Hunter wanted to ask him what he was going to do to get these answers, but he wasn't sure he wanted him to tell him it was going to be simple. Nothing so far with this woman was simple. Hunter stood up when he did.

"You'll leave her alone while I try to find this out for you. I mean completely. No more emails and no more hanging out at her house. You're better than that." He nodded and started to ask how long when his dad spoke again. "I'll have something for you by the end of the week. In the meantime, I want you to find us a place to stay that doesn't have us falling all over each other and has more than one bathroom."

Hunter didn't want to find a house for them. He wanted to see what his dad did. But he was his dad, and it mattered little that Hunter was nearly thirty-three years old. He still deserved his respect if nothing else.

~~~

The email didn't surprise her, but the person it was from did. She knew of Cash Emerson...few people didn't know him. She read the email twice before she burst out laughing. So the daddy was asking for the boy. Slone laughed while she went out to pick the tomatoes she was planning to freeze today.

It took her more than an hour to pick all the ripe fruit and another one to lay them out to be washed, cutting off the bad places and stems as she went. She was thinking about the email when she should have been paying attention and cut her hand all the way to her wrist. Badly too. She was making her way to the house when one of the wolves came to stand in front of her.

"I'm going inside." He looked at the house, then at her. "You can't help me. You know that. Just go and watch over the gates, please, and I'll be fine."

He followed her into the house, and she watched him as she rinsed off the wound. She could see the bone and felt her belly lurch up a bit before she wrapped her hand in the towel. She sat down and thought about what to do now.

She didn't heal like a regular wolf did, and that was why she was so careful when she worked. It would take nearly twice as long for her to heal from cuts as it did when she'd been human, too. She had no idea why but that's what happened. Even William had been surprised by that, thinking that she would have had the same abilities that all shifters did. He'd even taken her to a vet to find out what he could tell them. Of course, the man told the papers about how he'd treated the child of the murdered man and how she had been brought to him instead of a regular doctor. Thankfully, he had no idea why she'd been brought to him and they'd moved again. The motherfucker had even given them her picture, the one he'd gotten from his video surveillance cameras. It was one reason she hated people so much.

But she was bleeding, and she needed to think how to stop it. The wolf whined a little, and she looked at him. He was the most intelligent animal she'd ever met, and she was so jealous of him some days that she would hide from him when she went out so he'd not see how inadequate she was as a wolf.

"I might be better off dying here." He shook his head. "How the hell would you know? Are you just afraid that I'll die and you won't have any one to drop you meat so you don't have to leave the compound?"

He lay down on the floor and watched her. The towel around her hand was soaked through and she stood up to get another one, but dizziness made her fall back in the chair. He laid his head on her leg when she settled back down.

"Do you think you can find a man by the name of Cash Emerson?" She felt silly for asking him as if he knew anyone at all but her. "He seems like a nice enough man. He even told me that he thought his son was a horse's ass."

Slone ran her fingers over the wolf's dark coat. He watched her, but he didn't leave her. Finally, she had to lay her head down on the table and felt herself slipping off the chair. The next thing she knew, someone was picking her up.

"You can't walk on two legs." The man only lifted her higher in his arms. "Why are you here?"

"Your friend came to find me." She felt the bed touch her back and she knew she was dreaming. "I'm going to stitch up your hand now. Do you have anything to numb the pain?"

"No." He moved out of her vision and then back again in a few seconds. At least she thought it was only that long. But he was bent over her hand before she could ask him. He started talking before she could ask him how he'd gotten in her fence, much less her house.

"You don't have to worry none, darlin'. I won't tell them how I got in. Not that they'd believe me anyway. That wolf of yours, never seen a wild one so smart before. He was standing outside my room when I came home from dinner. Sniffed me right up and then took my hand in his mouth. Thought for sure he was going to have a snack of me."

"He's never bitten me before, so I think you're safe. I think he's like the Alpha to the rest of them." She felt the gauze being wrapped around her hand as he laughed. "How did you get in here?"

"The back end of your property is a cove. Did you know that?" She did and nodded. "Well, there is a nice cave along the side of the landscape and in it is a tunnel. It opens up right near your shed of all places."

"And you found this because of the wolf." The man nodded and stood up. She was feeling slightly off still and didn't get up. There was no reason to show him how weak she was. But she would have to be more careful about her entrance to the compound. The only other person, before today, who knew about the cave at the shoreline was the guy who made deliveries for her. And William, when he brought her things she'd ask for. She'd have to make sure she locked her end from now on. And for all she knew, he was.... "Who the hell are you, anyway?"

"Cash Emerson." Stunned, Slone looked at the wolf who was seated next to her bed. "Yeah, I think he knew which one of us to get, too. I don't know how he figured it out, but here I am. Don't even know how he figured out I was here yet."

"I told him." Cash nodded, not the least bit surprised, it seemed, that she'd told the wild wolf to go and find him for her. "The rest of your family, they'll be coming in soon, too, I suppose."

"Nope. I don't see any reason for them to know that I was even here." He sat on the chair across from her and smiled. "You're not at all what I expected, Miss Morris."

Slone waited for him to say more and when he didn't she sat up on the side of the bed and looked around the room. There was nothing in here to show who she really was, as there was nothing in the rest of the house either. She looked down at the wolf when she spoke to the man.

"I don't know how you know what it is you think you do, but I just want to be left alone. I've not bothered anyone in town and, contrary to your son's thoughts about me, I'm not out to bilk the town out of anything either. I'm just...." She felt the tears threaten and wanted to cry. But years ago she'd learned that it never solved anything and people had more things to use against her when she did.

"You don't look like the little girl you were back then. Your hair is the same color, but that's about it. You do look like your dad a little. I think it's the eyes. But that's not it either." He leaned forward as he continued. "I saw the scars on your wrist and that's what gave you away."

Slone looked at the deep mark on her wrist. Like the ones on her belly and her butt, it had scarred over when it healed. She pulled her sleeve down over it and looked at the man. It was on the tip of her tongue to tell him he was wrong. But she found that she didn't want to lie to him. There was something so...something so kind about his face that she knew that she could and should trust him.

"They told me that they should have gone away, the marks, but they didn't." He nodded. "No one can understand why I never heal like a shifter, or why I have scars when their kind doesn't. William thinks it's because his dad didn't finish the process before he died. But he did save me from death."

"You wishing sometimes that he didn't?" She nodded but didn't say anything to him. "Thought so. Only a person who doesn't care about life anymore would hold up in a place like this. What would have happened had the wolf not come to find me?"

"I don't know. Before when I passed out from being hurt, I woke a few hours later. I'm very careful about when I hurt myself. This time...it was really deep, deeper than I thought."

"I would say that your body can't take keeping you up and about while it tries to heal you faster. So you sort of fade out so that it can do its thing. You are healing faster, just not as fast as, say, I would." He got up and looked at the blood soaking through the gauze.

"I'll have to change it again after you go." She put her hand behind her so that he'd not see it shake. She'd not had a conversation with a person in years, and she was a little off her game.

He laughed. "Is that your polite way of telling me to get lost?" Slone flushed. "I'm sorry. I wouldn't have come at all, but the wolf seemed to think you needed me."

"I don't have company." He nodded and smiled at her as he sat down. Slone sat as well, then stood up and moved to the kitchen. She was sure her intent was to show him out, but she was putting on a kettle for tea and getting down a tin of scones when he walked in and sat down at the table. "People won't leave me alone. I mean, I don't know what they want with me. I'm not bothering anyone."

"Perhaps that's why." She nodded and pulled down two plates she'd made when she'd been going through a pottery stage in her loneliness. He picked up the sort of round plate and smiled before setting it down. "My son seems to think you're running drugs from here, or you have the world's largest meth lab going. I have no idea where he developed these major distrust issues. I think the two of you would suit."

"I don't...men don't want me." He frowned but said nothing. "I don't know why talking to you is so easy. You...I usually have problems even putting two words together about people. Especially men."

"Did a man hurt you?" She shook her head. "Then why do you hide here? You have an entire pack that would welcome you."

"My money, you mean." She flushed again. "I'm sorry. I shouldn't say things like that. It's just that I want to be left alone. I feel better when I'm just by myself."

"The wolves to keep you company, you mean." They both looked over at the one that had gone to get Cash. "He is very devoted to you. I would say that he runs with you when you go out."

"No. You'd be wrong." She stood up then, and he did as well. When he started to speak, she cut him off. "I'm very sorry, Mr. Emerson, it's time you left. If you wouldn't mind not telling anyone how you got here, I'd very much appreciate it. And tell your son to back off. I'm not going to play his games."

Cash stared at her for several seconds. Then he nodded. Taking another scone from the plate, he turned to leave. She followed him to the shed entrance and stood there while he moved into the opening. But he turned to her at the last moment.

"You won't be happy here now. You've had a taste of companionship and you'll want more. If you do...." He handed her his cell phone and stepped back. "Call me. My number is under the phone information. And I'm staying at the hotel in town for now."

He disappeared before she could say anything else or even give him back his phone. Putting it in her pocket to toss out later, she locked the door and looked at the wolf. He was cocking his head at her as if he, too, didn't understand why she was hiding out.

"No more visitors, if you please." He stared a little longer before he snorted at her and left. Slone moved to finish with the tomatoes. She had a lot to do today and having tea and scones shouldn't have been on the list. But she had a feeling that Cash was right. She'd be lonelier now.

Chapter 3

Hunter looked at the trucks in the yard of the house. He and his brothers had made a list just yesterday when their dad had finally come back to the hotel. The guys moving in and out of the building looked like they were on a mission and damn the person or people that got in their way. He walked to who he thought was in charge.

"Hunter Emerson." The man took his outstretched hand, and Hunter knew he was a wolf as well. "You know who called you in today?"

"Miss Giles. She said we had a week to bring this up to code and she'd give us a fat bonus. Wonderful woman, Miss Giles. She also told me she'd use us for all the construction she needed from now on, too." He looked at the house as he continued. "The name is Rogers, Dan Rogers. This place was shit, if you don't mind me saying so."

"It was." They both watched as two men, both wolves, picked up several bags of grout and moved into the house. "We're tiling the kitchen floor as well as the five bathrooms. The showers are coming in later today. You have a preference on what the color might be?"

"Not really." He moved into the house with Dan just as a pallet of drywall was being lifted to the upper level. Hunter had never seen so many men on one site for a single project in his life. He asked Dan about it.

"I have a medium-sized firm...well, getting to be large. I called some men off a few other projects and called in some favors. Still don't know if I'll make the deadline or not. But most of these guys can really use the money."

"We work construction at home. We could help out." Dan looked at him suspiciously. "I swear to you it's not anything that's running in your head right now. We were going to work on it anyway. There is no way we can stay in the hotel for much longer. There are seven of us, counting my dad, and we'll be on top of each other."

"You're Emerson Builders." Hunter nodded. "Why didn't she just ask you to do it? I mean, you are the Alpha, right?"

"I don't know. But I intend to find out." Three vehicles pulled up just as they were coming out of the house. His dad looked at him like he had a secret, and Hunter felt his wolf stir. As they made the introductions, his dad moved off to speak to Dan while the foreman came and told them where they were most needed. In twenty minutes, they were all working on their new house.

Lee and Graham were both in the same room he was and they were all working quietly. When he helped Lee lift a sheet of walling into place, Graham hit it with the screws and they were on the second one when their dad came into the room. He leaned against the wall to watch, and Hunter looked at him.

"Spill it, old man. You've been walking around like you have some secret since last night. What has you looking like a cat that just ate the canary?" His dad moved to take the screwdriver from Graham and sent him for some water. Lee left a few seconds later to get another box of screws. They were alone.

"I met her." It took Hunter a few seconds to realize what he meant. "She's not running drugs and not growing them either. She's just a woman who likes to be alone, and she makes the best scones I've ever eaten. Here, try this and tell me what you think."

Hunter looked at the cookie in his Baggie. It was blueberry, his favorite, and he wanted it in the worst kind of way. But he held off, thinking there was a trick. He eyed his dad.

"You met her how? And if you did, where? She never comes out of that fortress of hers." He finally took the Baggie and opened it. The scent nearly took his breath away. "She made this?"

"She did. She, of course, didn't say she did, but I know a fresh scone when I see one. And I had a cup of tea with her, too. After I stitched up her hand, of course." Hunter nearly choked on the scone. He was taking in big gulps of air as he tried his best to dislodge the crumb that had taken up residence in the back of his throat. When he could finally talk, his voice was hoarse from it.

"You expect me to believe you had a little tea party with the woman who for all intents and purposes hasn't had any contact with another person in years? And what do you mean you 'stitched up her hand'? What the hell did you do to her?" His dad just glared. "I'm sorry, but that's about as farfetched as I've ever heard from you."

"I found her passed out on the floor of her kitchen in a puddle of blood. She'd cut her hand pretty badly, and I put her to bed. She must have—"

"What the hell are you talking about?" His dad cocked a brow at him, and Hunter realized how loud he'd been. "Dad, how did you manage to do what most of the people around here would give their left nut for? And you were in her bedroom?"

"She's very hurt, son. I mean not just from the cut, but her mind and heart are...I don't know if she'll ever recover from it." Hunter could see that his dad was moved by this woman, but knew that it was more than likely a scam she was playing. It wasn't until he continued that Hunter knew his dad was telling the truth. "She was hurt as a child and converted without her knowledge. It was that or die, and the wolf who changed her did it at great risk to himself. He even died a few hours later for what he did to save her."

"You knew him then." He nodded, and Hunter sat down on the paint can. "When did this happen?"

"I'm sorry, Hunter, but I can't tell you anymore. The only reason I told you this was so you'd leave her alone. She's...I would say that she's happy where she is and that whatever you think she's doing over there, she's not. Miss Mo...Miss Giles is simply living alone and doing nothing to bother any of us." He sat down and looked at him. "She has my cell phone. I gave it to her in the event she got hurt again or just needed to talk to someone. There is no one there but her and her wild pack of wolves."

Lee and Graham came back a couple of minutes later, and they worked on the room until they had the walls hung and the tape in place. Jarrett would come in and seal the tape, and Luke would do the ceilings. It was the way he'd been working construction sites since he was a kid. Dan found him in the third bedroom just after noon.

"You guys know how to work together. I might have to let you organize my own men in that sort of work.

Never had a team get so much done in such a short amount of time before." Hunter smiled and told him he would help in any way he could. "Also, I wanted to ask you if scale was fine for you. That's what we're paying the rest of the men."

"We aren't a part of your crew, Dan, so we don't expect to get paid at all. We just needed to work off some energy, and this was a way to do it." Dan started to shake his head. "I'm serious. We all have enough to live on, and we barged in on your crew. We enjoyed it."

Graham nodded, as did Lee. Smiling, Dan moved out of the house with them and to the long tables that had been set up for lunch. He looked at all the women who were bringing bowls of food from trucks and cars.

"Miss Giles again. She did this the last time we worked for her. Pete calls them in and gives them some money from her and they organize and execute in no time. The only thing we have to do is set up the tables and wash our hands before we sit down." Hunter had never seen so much food in his life and said as much to Dan. "Yeah, they do know how to cook, these women. It's one of the perks of working here. These people know how to take care of their own."

He ate until he thought he'd bust. Hunter was still shoveling food in his mouth as pies were brought to the table. Christ, if he didn't gain any weight from this, he'd be surprised. And when he bit into a slice of the lemon custard, he moaned and looked at his dad when he laughed.

"This is what life is all about." He nodded. "I think I could get used to this. We having this sort of thing at the pack meeting Friday?"

"I hope." The woman who was pouring him more coffee grinned at him when he looked at her. "We used to have them every meeting, but we sort of got away from it. The townspeople have been less than...well, let's just say they don't take kindly to us having a full moon party like animals. That old mayor, the one they had just before this one, had been biting at the bit to get over here and run us off. But Miss Giles, she kept him in line. Last time he threatened us, she had a bunch of lawyers come in and look over his books. He was out before the plan cooled off. But this new guy, he's not much better."

Hunter looked at his dad when the woman moved away. She'd made sure he knew her name and her phone number because, as she told him, she was the head honcho when it came to the food. His dad only shook his head.

"You think we need to talk to him, too?" His dad shrugged, and Hunter leaned back in his chair. "There something else I need to know about our benefactor?"

"I would say that there's plenty you should know, but I'm not going to tell you. I made a promise and you know me well enough to understand, I don't take those lightly."

"I do. But you have to know me well enough to know that I can't let her keep paying for everything and not getting something in return. And I understand that her privacy is all she wants. But even you have to admit that she's going to undermine me if she keeps stepping in like this."

"Perhaps what you should ask yourself, Hunter, is this: is she undermining you or is she helping you?" He got up and left him there. Hunter took out his cell phone and did something he promised himself he wouldn't do when his dad told him he'd given her his phone. He called the mystery woman.

~~~

The phone ringing startled her. She'd not heard one in years, and she stared at the thing for a good minute before she looked at the caller ID. Hunter was all it said, and she knew from the emails that she'd been getting from Luke that he was the new Alpha. She put the phone back down and worked on the rest of her order to the grocery store.

She got in supplies once a month from one of the large warehouses in another city. They would bring it to William's house, and he'd bring it out to her on the boat. They would visit for a time when he did it, sometimes bringing Jess and their four children, but they never came to her house. Slone had invited them but they never accepted. Instead, they'd play on the beach and have a lovely picnic. And as it would be cold soon, she had to order enough to last her until spring. That would be four months' worth of supplies. By the time she was finished, the phone had rang six more times.

Hunter had to know that his dad had given her his phone. Why she still had it was beyond her. She was never going to call him, but Slone found that she didn't want to toss it like she'd thought she would. And yesterday, while she'd been bringing in the last of her brussels sprouts, she'd actually looked for the older gentleman.

By the time she was coming in for the night, she'd had nine more phone calls from the man and he'd left messages, too. Those, she couldn't retrieve because she didn't have the pin number, but she doubted that she would have anyway. They would be, no doubt, just like his email, sort of cruel while being rude, too. But the man was driving her crazy. Just as she lifted the cover of the phone to turn it off, it rang, and she inadvertently answered it.

"Hello?" She felt her hair on her arms dance and knew that he was as surprised as she was that she'd answered. "Miss Giles? Are you there?"

"What do you want?" He didn't speak for several seconds, and she thought maybe he'd hung up. But his breathing told her otherwise. "Why are you calling me? I thought I made it perfectly clear that I didn't want to be bothered."

"You have. But things are going on that I need to have some information on. Like this house you're having renovated for us. What gives you the right to go in and take over like that?" She started to answer, but he cut her off. "And since when do you take on the local government and get mayors fired? That is not part of your job. It's not even part of the pack's interference."

"First and foremost, the building belongs to me. If I want to have it set on fire and dance around it naked, it's well within my rights. What's the problem? You think I should have hired the great and powerful Emerson Builders to do the job? Dan and his crew needed the money and the experience; you do not. As for the mayor? Fuck off. When he started telling the people of the pack that they had to go to another city for their staples as well as the fact that he doubled my taxes on the property, I stepped in. And yes, before you ask me, I have plans already in the works to have this bastard taken out as well. Did you know that six of your pack have been fired from their jobs because of the idiotic list he's put together?"

Slone took a deep breath and was startled to hear him laughing. Not just a short one either, but she imagined him to be rolling with it. And she thought he sounded like he'd been laughing for a while, too. "What the hell is so funny?"

"You. I've never gotten a woman's panties in a twist so fast in my life. Christ, I bet you can take on about anyone you set your mind to, can't you?" She didn't answer him but stood looking at the bowl of batter she'd been mixing for fresh scones. Then as if he'd been reading her mind, he mentioned them. "I had one of your scones the other day. If you can bake like that and keep the pack in line, I might just marry you."

"You most certainly will not." He laughed again, and she felt her temper snap. "Listen, buddy, since you know that your father gave me his phone, you knew who you were calling. I want you to stop bothering me right now. I have to get ready for things and I don't have time to be social with you."

"I'd very much like to meet you. Just for the simple fact that I can almost see you now in my mind and want to equate the woman with the dream. Are you by any chance a redhead? I dearly love redheads." She looked at her reflection in the door glass and her red hair. She shivered when he continued talking. "My dad said he saw you. That's not terribly fair of you to see him and not me. Don't you think?"

Slone sat down. If she didn't know any better she'd say he was flirting with her. But men did not flirt with women like her. At least not after they saw her. She wasn't going to let him seduce her, not that he really could.

"Look, Mr. Emerson, I've told you repeatedly that I want to be left alone. I have no desire to be a part of your pack, or anyone's for that matter. I like being alone." He didn't say anything, so she continued, "I have my life just the way I like it, and I wish for you to leave me alone."

"I'm afraid I can't do that." She started to ask him why not when he laughed again. "I can't work with my pack if you're going to be a major stepping stone for me. I need to meet with you so that we can iron out what is your responsibility and mine. Right now, we are at a crossroads, you and I."

"Why?" He asked her what she meant. "Why is it important that you meet with me? I can have my attorney contact you if you want to iron out what you think you need to. But I'm not going to come to you. It's just not…I don't do people well."

"Then I'm afraid you've left me no choice." She listened to the tone for several seconds before she realized that he'd hung up on her. Laying the phone down, she went to her computer to email her attorney. She gave him an outline of the conversation she'd had with the new Alpha as well as what she'd done. Twenty minutes later, he emailed her back.

You should meet with him. I know that you've no desire to do so, but it might make this go away for you. I could set up a meeting here in my office and make sure that there are no other people around. Just you and him and me if you'd like. I know that what you are doing for the pack is what needs to be done, but he will not stop. I've known Hunter for a long time, and he is nothing if not persistent.

Slone finished the scones as she thought about what he'd told her. If she met with him on her turf she'd be finished with him and she could move on with her life. Not that she wanted to go to the city again—she'd not been there in years—but she knew that if she went, she could see about getting a new freezer as well as a few other things that she needed. A tractor for one. As she took the last of the baked goods out of her oven, she sat down. It was time to finish this.

Set it up, but make sure that he brings his father along with him. And no one else. I will do this on my terms, not his. He told her he'd set it up as soon as possible.

Also, could you please find me a place to go for a few supplies? I will enclose the list when you tell me he has agreed to my terms. Some of the things I will need are as follows. The list wasn't all that long, but she'd thought about a few other things while she'd been baking. If she got even half of it, she'd be thrilled and she might not have to make another trip for another seventeen years. Going to bed, she lay there and thought of the trial and the media when she'd been found to be sole heir to her mother's fortune.

The headlines had been vicious. Whatever thing they could think of, they had printed. And the wounds on her body had been printed and reprinted so much that she'd finally had to sue a few papers to get them to stop. As the anniversary of her parents' death approached, she was seeing more and more about her again. Why wouldn't they simply leave her alone? Lying in the bed and looking out the window, she thought about the meeting with the Alpha. It would be her first, and she was going to make sure it was the last. This had to stop as well.

"Perhaps I should just buy some island and live there until I die. That way I could live in some sort of peace and not have to worry about who was doing what to whom." Rolling to her back, she thought of her dad, the only man she'd ever loved.

He'd been so good to her before Eva had come into their lives. Slone's mother had died when she'd been born so she never knew her. But her daddy she did. They were inseparable. And he'd taken her on outings that were the best adventures. And then he'd met Eva.

Slone would admit that she'd liked the woman, too. At first. She'd been kind to her and her dad, cooking and cleaning up their house. Then when her dad asked Slone if she'd be okay with her being her step-mom, she'd been thrilled. But as soon as the ring was on Eva's finger, things took a terrible twist for Slone. Slone was four when they married, and her life had changed so much that she had nightmares to this day about them.

"She's winning." Slone smiled at the sound of her voice in the big room. "I know that, but it doesn't change the fact that she still haunts my dreams. And will more than likely do it forever." Closing her eyes, Slone wiped at the useless tears and tried to sleep. As soon as she met with the Alpha, she was going to make sure no one hurt her again.

The dream took her almost immediately. She almost welcomed it as the fear took away some of the pain. But as she stood on the large stone and watched the water move by her, all Slone could think about was that it began and ended right there.

"Get in." She looked at her stepmother not in fear, because this was only a dream, but as someone who was seeing a well-loved movie, this one full of horror, for the hundredth time. Only she didn't love it...the nightmare twisted her up inside until she could hardly breathe sometimes. "Get in the water, Slone, and drown this time. I have no use for you, and I don't want you stepping on my toes again."

The voice changed then and became the voice she'd heard on the phone tonight. "You're not in my dream. Go away and leave me alone."

"No. I'm going to have my way and you're going to give me everything. I want you to be gone from here so I can have everything." She asked him what he wanted. "Well, you dead for starters. Didn't you understand that when your stepmother tossed you in the water? You're not welcome around here. We all just want you dead."

He grabbed her around the neck, and she felt the air being cut off. The harder she clawed at him to breathe, the more he laughed. She was just feeling her vision start to fade when he let her go. Screaming, Slone sat up in her bed to hear the wolves outside the house howling. Shivering, she got up and looked out. They were there in the moonlight, all of them. And her buddy was staring right at her.

"It was just a dream." She told herself that over and over as she stepped into the shower. "It was just a dream." But the marks on her throat, where her nails had dug deep into her flesh when she'd been fighting with the faceless man, made her think it was more than a dream and maybe a premonition. A premonition of what, she had no idea, but it probably wasn't good.

She knew it would be pointless to try to go back to bed and sat at her computer to move some stocks around. When she heard back from her attorney an hour later, she saw that she was to meet him the day after tomorrow. She wondered what the Alpha would think of the woman behind the fence.

Chapter 4

Hunter would have to admit that having a private jet sent for him wasn't anything that he'd expected. And having a woman there waiting on them hand and foot was kind of nice, too. If they were surprised that all seven of them were coming, they gave no indication of that either, but kept them content on the two-hour flight. It wasn't until they were in the air that he thought to ask where their hostess was.

"Miss Giles is already in town, sir. She had some things she needed to care for before the meeting." He nodded and took the glass of water from her. Lee was flirting with the other woman, but she was ignoring him like he was a small boy. It made Hunter laugh to see him so frustrated. Lee apparently wasn't used to having women do that to him.

"Do you suppose she pays them to be professional like that?" Hunter looked at his dad when he spoke. "I've never seen a more polite couple of stewardesses in my life. And if you asked them for a steak, I bet they'd have the plane land to get it for you."

"No doubt. It makes me wonder how much this woman is really worth." His dad just nodded. "Dad, I'm going to meet her in a couple of hours. Don't you think you can tell me something about her?"

"You're going to see her in a few hours, but I doubt you'll actually get to meet her." He started to ask him what the hell the difference was when Dad shook his head. "You'll see. I'm betting right now that this meeting wasn't her idea, and that you'll come out of it with less than you want and a good deal more than you'd hoped for."

Hunter stared at his dad. "Why don't you have your head examined while we're here? I'm pretty sure you've lost your mind. I don't have a clue what the hell you're talking about."

Before his dad could say anything, the pilot came on the line. "Please fasten your seatbelts, gentlemen. We are going to be landing in four minutes. The weather in New York is sixty-three degrees, with a slight wind. Also, there will be a limo awaiting you when we are free to disembark. Two have been sent to accommodate the extra guests. Mr. Connor will be there to meet you."

He looked at his dad, and he shrugged. Connor was the attorney he'd spoken to on the phone several times over the past few days. Hunter wondered when they were going to meet with Miss Giles.

The man standing at the end of the long carpet moved toward them. He was expensive was all that Hunter could think of, and he wore it well. When he took his hand, Hunter was surprised to find out he was human. Hunter tried to think how to ask him about it when the man laughed.

"We all are that work for Miss Morris. She has made sure that we're all aware of what she is and that we are up on pack laws as well." He nodded to the first limo. "If you'd not mind riding with me, Mr. Emerson, as well as your father, your brothers will be taken to the hotel. Miss Morris will be at my office. And since you have both signed off on the nondisclosure forms, we can get right to work."

"Miss Morris?" Hunter took the file from the man as soon as he asked about the name change. "If we're meeting with someone other than Miss Giles, I'm going to be really pissed. This has been really nice and all, but I didn't come all this way to meet with a representative."

"Miss Morris is her name. Giles is the name of the family that took her in when she was a child. In that file you'll see why all the cloak and dagger is happening. Miss Morris does not want the media to find her again."

He opened the file to a picture of a child. She was beautiful to say the least and her smile was breathtaking. Hunter wasn't sure what was going on until he flipped the picture over to see the headlines of a newspaper clipping. Then as quick as that, everything fell into place.

"She's the billionaire heiress." Mr. Connor nodded. "Christ, no wonder she wanted her privacy. I don't even know her and I would more than likely be doing the same thing. Dad, did you know this?"

"I did. Not immediately, mind you, but once I saw her wrist, I knew as well." His dad hadn't opened his file but looked at the attorney. "How is she? I hope much better than the last time I saw her."

"She is. And I have to tell you, I'm impressed." Mr. Connor leaned back in the seat. "Do you know that you're the first person that has seen her in over ten years? Apart from her guardian and those wolves of hers. She also made you some scones. She said you had taken a liking to them."

His dad just smiled and sat back. The man couldn't have spent more than a couple of hours with her and

Hunter could see he was smitten. As he looked over the file, his unease at what he had done to this woman increased tenfold. By the time the car came to a smooth stop, he was feeling pretty shitty.

"I don't think I should have done this." Mr. Connor nodded. "Is she upset? Is this meeting going to be nothing but a shouting match between the two of us?"

"I would say that's a good bet. Miss Morris does not like to be shoved into a corner, and you have pushed her over her limits. If she was willing to have this meeting with you, I'm betting she'll want something in return. And I have a feeling you're not going to like it." Hunter had a feeling he wasn't either. "I would do as she asks, Mr. Emerson. Not to sound threatening, but she is used to getting what she wants and she has enough money to back it up. And when I left her to come to see you, she wasn't really in the best of humor. Something about some shipments that aren't going her way."

"Shipments?" His mind automatically went to nefarious things. "What sort of shipments is she having brought into my pack?"

Connor laughed and said nothing as he got out of the car. His dad smacked him in the back of the head, and he nearly glared at him but thought he'd live longer if he didn't.

"You are forever the most suspicious man I've ever known when it comes to this woman. Why is that, I wonder? Has she treated you badly in another life? Shit in your oatmeal? What is about her that has you acting like a fool?"

Instead of embarrassing himself more, he simply got out of the limo as well. And nearly got back inside. The building was impressive to say the least, and the name on the front of it had him swallowing twice before he looked at Connor.

"Morris Enterprises?" Connor nodded. "Mother fuck, I'm so screwed, aren't I? I should just tuck my tail between my legs and go home now."

"If you do, you will piss her off more. If I were you, I'd go in, tell her what it is you want, and then listen to what she wants. She may be pissed, Mr. Emerson, but she's not unreasonable. At least not where the pack is concerned."

Hunter moved into the building and was handed an identification badge, complete with his picture already on it. Hunter looked at the picture that was the same as the one on his driver's license and wondered at the pull this woman had if she could do this. He looked at his dad.

"I'm so fucked right now." His dad laughed, which was not encouraging. "What should I do?"

"I would say keep your mouth shut, but we both know that's not going to happen. What I would do is be as much myself as...no, that won't work for you either." His dad eyed him as they moved toward the elevator. "I think you might be right, son. You're very fucked."

Yeah, he thought, *I should have listened to my family.*

~~~

Slone wasn't sure what to do with her hands. And her hair was a mess. She should have gotten it cut. It had been years since she'd seen the inside of a hair salon. Slone had been chopping at her own hair for the last ten years, and she was afraid it looked it. Then there were her clothes. Why she'd even packed this skirt was beyond her. Slone was, in a word, a mess.

The conversation that she'd had with the salesman at the lawn and garden place had made her mad. She should have known better than to ask to speak to the manager.

She was a woman, after all, and what did they know of farm equipment? Then when she'd finally convinced him that what she wanted was what she wanted, he'd laughed at her when she told him she wanted to take it back on a plane with her. Today. Slone decided that she hated men. All of them. When the elevator dinged, she looked up. Terror made her look for somewhere to hide.

The first person she saw was Shawn, her lawyer. The next was Cash Emerson. All her fears and anxiety seemed to dissipate in that moment. Then the man behind him stepped off. Slone took two steps back. She had no idea he was so big.

"Miss Morris, it's good to see you again." Cash stepped in front of her and took her chin into his hand. "Breathe, dear, it's going to be fine. Just breathe."

Nodding, she watched his face. It was better than the scowling man behind him. When she felt she could look up again, she saw that the younger Emerson had sat down. She moved to the other side of the room to try and control her shakes. Shawn came to stand near her.

"Would you like to go into my office?" She nodded, then shook her head. "You can do this, honey. Just go over and stand if you have to. And if you never sit down, I think they'll understand."

"What did you tell them?" He said nothing more than she allowed. "He's so huge. I mean bigger than my dad."

"He is." Shawn stood near her as the other two sat at the long conference table. She wanted to get this over with but felt the terror of being exposed race along her spine again. As she made her way to the table, she moved to the end that was as far from the other two as possible. She stood there thinking she should explain.

"I'm not good with people." She expected a laugh or at least someone to snort. "I've been on my own for a long time and I thought I could handle this better. I'm not...I used to...."

"You're doing fine." Cash smiled as he continued. "If you need to sit down there, I'm sure we can hear each other. And before we begin, I'd like to tell you how incredibly sorry I am. I wish now that I'd just told this ass that I'd gotten an email from you and not met you."

"I wish you would have just left me alone." She felt the tears fill her eyes and her temper start to rise. "I was doing just fine on my own, and everybody was fine with it."

"Maybe, but you were doing things to undermine what I was trying to do as Alpha. I was going to see how things were, and you had to step in and—" She cut him off when Hunter paused.

"And what? Clean up a building that needed to be set to right? A building that belonged to me." He mumbled something, and she snapped at him. "What did you say?"

"I said that you always fall back on that, don't you? The wealthy and powerful Slone Morris will make sure that people will come to her rather than their Alpha when things are going wrong. Or if you stub your toe, she'll make sure that you have all the coverage you need." He stood up and leaned on the table as he continued. "You just couldn't sit back and let me do my job, could you? You had to have the last word on it all."

"What the hell are you talking about?" She glanced at Cash as he pulled at his son's shirt. "You're the most pompous ass I've ever met. Why don't you go back to where you came from?"

He came around the table to her and she was just too pissed to care. When he was standing in front of her, she lifted her chin to him and glared at him. There was so much fire in his eyes that she was mesmerized by them. When he pulled her body to his, hip to hip, and lifted her up, she nearly cried out, but his mouth came down on hers. It was so forceful and quick that she put her arms around his shoulders before she could think she should have pushed at him to let her go.

He lifted his head from hers but not by much. Slone had never been kissed before. Not by any man like this one. When he lowered his head again, taking her lower lip into his mouth, she could only grip his shoulders tighter as he rolled his hips into hers.

"Do you know what you are to me?" She shook her head as he whispered to her. His mouth was doing incredible things to her and she wanted more. "Mate? You're my mate. Do you know what that means?"

Her body seemed to come alive at his words. She struggled to pull from him and he let her go, but he didn't back off. She moved back from him as far as the wall and tried to get her mind to function again. She was not going to be his mate, not any man's.

"You have to go. I won't bother you anymore if you do the same for me." He moved to within a foot of her and she put up her hands. "I don't want you here. Please, you can't want me as a mate. I don't...I'm not even sure that this isn't some ploy to get what you want. Or money. Is that it?" She looked up at him as he started cursing.

"No, I don't want your fucking money. But if you think this is just going to go away, then you're more naive than I thought. The only reason I pissed you off before was because you looked ready to jump out of your skin. And when I smelled you, it was all I could do not to throw you on the table and take you." She looked at the table, and he growled. "If you don't behave yourself, you're going to find yourself flat on your back and me buried deep inside of you now."

"Hunter?" They both turned to look at Cash. His face was alight with humor, and she wanted to smack him, too. "I think that we've gotten off track here. Perhaps we should let you two settle this in a more private setting."

"No." She nearly screamed at him, and Cash laughed then. He looked at her and nodded. "No. There is nothing to settle here. We're done. Right now, we're done. I'll leave you alone and you'll not hear another thing from me. I'll sign over the buildings to you as well. Just…I want to leave now."

"You're not going anywhere." Almost as soon as the words left Hunter's mouth, she felt her wolf stir. He grabbed her arms and shook her. "Calm her or she'll pull mine. And I'm pretty sure that your pretty offices will not take two mating wolves the way I want you right now."

"Please don't do this." He pulled her into his arms, and she felt the weight of the last two days take her under. Slone was sobbing so hard that she had to sit down with her head between her knees. All she could see was the feet of Hunter. After a few more minutes, she sat up. He sat in the chair across from her. She noticed that the other two men were gone.

"I sent them out. My dad is no doubt calling my brothers right now, and Mr. Connor said something about a meeting with a company called Plow It Under. Are you planning to have me buried?" She knew he was joking, but she wasn't in the mood.

"Not yet." He nodded and watched her like she was going to explode. "Why did you say those things to me? If you think being rude to me is the way to control me, you were right. But I'm better now. I'm not a pushover most of the time, but today…you caught me off guard."

"You might think you are, but I'm having a hard time believing that. You had no problems standing up to me just now. And I didn't lie to you. You're my mate. What do you know about that?" She wanted to pace. Slone really wanted to go home, but she could see that he wasn't going to let her. She looked at him when he said her name.

"I was raised by a pair of wolves. Born, not made. The man who converted me, his son and daughter-in-law raised me. They told me some…not a lot, but some of what happens to me once a month, but for the most part they left me alone. I know what a mate is." She looked at him. "I'm not willing to be your mate, no matter what. And I'm pretty sure that once you think about it, you'll see why this is a dumb idea."

"And why is that?" She did stand to pace then, and he moved his feet so she could. Her heart was still pounding in her chest, but she wasn't as wobbly as she'd been before. He didn't say anything to her as she made several passes, and she wondered if she could get out of the room before he could stop her.

"I wouldn't if I were you. Not only would I catch you, but my wolf would surface. And I wasn't kidding when I told you he'd take you right now. In fact, I'm having a hard time just controlling me around you, much less the wolf." She turned to look at him and could see his wolf run along his arms. She felt her own respond to his. "You're not making this very easy. Please either sit down or come here so that I can touch you."

"I'm not going to do either. You have to get this notion out of your head right now. I'm not going to be your mate." She started pacing again. "I'm not...I don't want someone in my life. Especially someone like you."

"And what is it about me that you don't want?" He sounded like he was purring at her, and she paced harder. "Come here, Slone, and let me touch you, please?"

"You have to know from the file that Shawn gave you that I'm not going to be a nice person to you. I'm barely nice to him. And I can't have you touching me. I don't care for being touched. Not at all. I get the willies when I'm touched." She was babbling and wasn't sure how she'd started doing that, but couldn't seem to stop. "I'm also damaged, too. You should see my body. I was hurt when Willie saved me. And the scars are horrific. Even I hate to look at them."

He was suddenly behind her, and he wrapped his arms around her waist. Every part of her wanted to run. And every part of her wanted to lean back into him as well. She felt his hand move up her arm, pulling the sleeve with him. She closed her eyes when he exposed her.

"He bit into your wrist. I can see his teeth marks here." His finger moved over the small punctures gently, and her breath caught. When he lifted it to his mouth and licked along them, she felt as if he'd run his tongue over her entire body. "Where else did he bite you?"

"My belly." He pulled her blouse out of her skirt, and she tried to pull it back down, but he wouldn't allow that and lifted it to just below her bra. Turning her around, he dropped to his knees and did the same thing to the bite marks on her waist, both front and back. "You can see that I'm messed up badly. They don't even think I can have children. They said...he told me...the doctor told me I'd never be able to get pregnant."

She moaned when he nipped at her navel, then swirled his tongue in the indentation. She put her hand on his head and curled her fingers into his hair. The silkiness of it made her run her fingers from the front to the back before she gripped him again.

"Where else?" His voice was harsh, hoarse with need. She knew that if she could have spoken, she would sound just the same. And right now, the thought of him taking her was making her dizzy with need. "Where else did he bite you, Slone? Tell me."

"He didn't...not a bite mark. He clawed me to hold me." She lifted her skirt for him, and he pulled her panties down. "He held me so that the current wouldn't take me away."

Hunter bit her there. His teeth sank into her muscle so hard that she cried out with it. When he turned her back around to him, he buried his face into the apex of her thighs and inhaled deeply. Slone was so wet she was embarrassed by it.

"I need to taste you, Slone. I want to see if you taste as wonderful as you smell." He jerked her panties off her, and she cried out again when he nipped at her thigh. "Sit down on the table. I want to feel you come down my throat."

Her body was responding before her mind could come up with a reason why this was a bad idea. Hunter was between her legs, which he'd put on either side of his head before she could protest, if she was even going to. As soon as he pulled her clit into his mouth, she cried out his name and came. Never had anything made her feel this way.

He ate her like he was never going to stop. The more he took from her, the more he gave her, the more she wanted. Every time he bit down on her, she came, crying out his name. Every time he slid his tongue into her sheath, she knew she was soaking him. When he slid his fingers into her, she rode his hand, her hips coming up off the table like he was fucking her, and she realized that she wanted him to.

"Come for me again. Come and let me drink from you again." She lay back, her body so taut with need that when he sucked her clit into his mouth as he stretched her with his fingers, she bowed up off the table and screamed. He never stopped taking her even when she begged him to stop.

When he stood up over her, she could see that he'd released his cock. When she thought of him taking her, his thick cock entering her, Slone knew that it was going to hurt. But instead of sliding into her like they both wanted, he fisted his cock.

"I'm not going to take you the first time on a table in a conference room." He moaned when she reached for him. "Honey, you touch me and it's going to be over right now. I want to come all over you. Have my cum spray all over your pretty pussy until you come again. Tell me you want it. Tell me, Slone, tell me you want me."

"Please." He leaned over her and took her mouth. She could feel the head of his cock just at her entrance. When he bowed back, lifting his head from her, he roared out as he filled her, his cock slamming into her until she screamed with the pain. Over and over he took her hard, and she hurt. Hurt so badly that she wanted him to stop.

Hunter dropped over her and held her. His cock was still inside of her and she was afraid to move. She had no idea if she'd arouse him again so that he'd want to do it again, so she lay very still. When he lifted his head and looked down at her she turned her face away.

"Look at me, please." She didn't, and he said her name again. "Slone, look at me so I can see how badly I hurt you."

"I want you to get off me." He didn't move but chuckled a little. That had her looking at him. "You think this is funny? You hurt me. I know that I didn't put up any sort of fight, but you hurt me."

"And I'm profoundly sorry for that. But, Christ, woman, that was fantastic." She growled low at him, and he laughed again. "I could have you come again. Would that make you stay mad at me?"

She moved this time, and he stepped back. He stood before her, and she felt her body respond to his near nudity. Before she could do something really stupid, like beg him to bring her to climax again, she got up from the table and straightened her clothing.

"I want you again." She glared at him, and he laughed. "If you were honest with yourself, you'd say you wanted me, too. Only this time, we'd be better off in a bed. I could take you properly then."

Without a word, she went to the door and opened it. Before she stepped out into the empty hallway, he said her name. She turned to see him holding her panties in his fingers. When he took them to his nose and inhaled, Slone felt her knees weaken.

"This will have to do until next time." She left him then, slamming the door behind her. Slone made it all the way to the end of the hall before she realized she had no idea where she was going. A door behind her opened, and she dashed inside so quickly that the man who had come out leapt back. She locked the door and dropped to the floor. Sobbing, she tried to think what she had to do now.

Chapter 5

Hunter knew that his family could smell her on him. And right now he was more concerned about how badly he'd hurt her rather than what his family thought of him taking a mate. Finally finding her after all this time was something of a surprise. Finding out that it was a woman who despised him was something he'd never counted on. The drive to the restaurant was not long enough for him to figure things out. He started to get out behind his brothers, but his dad stopped him.

"Is she all right?" Hunter sat back on the seat and stared at his dad. He was going to be honest with him, but he didn't want to make him disappointed in him either.

"I honestly don't know. She is pissed, but I didn't take her against her will." His dad told him he never thought that. "I didn't mean to take her like I did. I only meant to...I didn't mean for any of that to happen. I've never needed a woman like I did her. Still want her if you want to know the truth. I could...Christ, Dad, I want to hunt her down and take her as many times as I can. Then do it again."

"You're both alphas. She may not realize it as yet, but she is as much as you are. What I meant was, is she all right with being your mate? I'm assuming not." Hunter shook his head. "I didn't think so. I tried to see her this afternoon and Shawn told me that she'd was indisposed. He said he was worried about her. He'd never seen her so upset before, he said."

"She thinks this will just go away." Hunter looked at the restaurant and thought of how empty it appeared. "She was really hurt by the other wolf. I...she showed me the scars. Why didn't they go away when she shifted the first time?"

"I don't know. She said the family she was staying with said that maybe Willie didn't finish the job before he died. Could be that. But she's going to have to come to understand that now that you've mated, there will be no going back to the way things were before." Hunter nodded. "You think she'll be here tonight?"

"I don't know. She's supposed to be. But after today, I really don't know." He looked at his dad. "I really hurt her. Not just physically, though that was enough, but I hurt her mentally, too. I never meant to take her that way. It was as if I had no control over myself concerning her needs."

"I'm sure they were met. She'd have killed you otherwise. But she's on the fragile side and a bit shy." Hunter flushed. "Want me to have a talk with her? She and I seemed to hit it off pretty good. And I never did get any of those scones she baked me."

Hunter thought about it and thought his dad would be the right person to talk to her. And he just realized that his wolf was fine with it as well. He looked at his dad. Hunter had an overwhelming urge to hug his dad then and reached for him. His dad patted him on the back as he returned the gesture.

"Please talk to her. I don't know what you can say to her, but please make her understand that I never meant to hurt her." His dad nodded and they both got out of the car. As soon as they entered the restaurant, Shawn met them at the door. This could not be good.

"She'd like a word with you after dinner, Mr. Emerson." Hunter nodded. "Good. And I have another request from her if you please. She wonders if you wouldn't mind not telling anyone what happened today. I have no idea what she means, but she was very determined that I ask you about it."

"I'm sure you don't but trust me, it's a wolf thing." He nodded, appearing somewhat relieved. They moved into the restaurant proper and noticed that there was no one else inside but them. And at six o'clock in the evening on a Friday, he was pretty sure they should have been hopping about now.

"She had them close for her." Hunter nodded. Of course she did. He moved to his seat as the waiter led them to a long table. He was seated at one end, and she was already seated at the other. He could see from where he was that she'd been crying, and he felt his heart twist a little more. His dad sat at her right and Shawn to her left.

Hunter didn't mind for now. She was in pain. Not just from the sex they'd had, because he knew that he'd hurt her, but because she was out of her element. And from the looks of things, so were his brothers. Lee leaned forward and looked at her.

"I wanted to welcome you to the family." She looked at him so quickly that Hunter knew she thought he'd told. Lee seemed to understand. "He didn't have to tell us, Slone. As a mated wolf, we can smell him on you. I'm sorry, I thought you knew that. I never meant to startle you."

"I didn't know. But thank you for telling me. And I'm not a part of your family, Mr. Emerson. I was merely in the wrong place at the wrong time." Hunter laughed, and she glared at him. "You have something to add, Mr. Emerson?"

"Yes." He picked up his wine glass that had just been filled and stood up. "To my future wife. May we have as much fun the rest of our lives as we had today."

Everyone at the table stared at the two of them. Slone stood up, and he was sure she was going to leave. Instead, she picked up her glass and raised it as he'd done.

"May you rot in hell for the rest of your life, you motherfucking asshole." As far as toasts went, it was bad, but she'd stood up to him, and he loved it. As soon as she sat down, his dad started clapping. Soon, the entire table was as well. Hunter nodded in her direction and took another sip of wine. As far as he was concerned, this was only the beginning. And as much as he wanted to spend his life with her, he also knew that she had to have some time to adjust. With a laugh, he decided that he'd give her an hour. Maybe two.

Dinner was wonderful. The conversation was even good after the first course was served, and once the ice had been broken, things moved well. Slone looked in his direction, but as discretely as possible.

Hunter had never enjoyed dressing up like this to eat, but was completely relaxed with it. He supposed it had to do with the company, but he thought it was finding her, too. She was simply perfect, even if she was a little on the intense side. He thought about what Jarrett had been about to find out about her and the day she'd been nearly killed.

"There's more on this one day of her life than I've ever seen on a person before. And about every five years or so, some dick shit gets it into his head to write another article. All of them are still looking for her for her side of the story." Jarrett handed him a few sheets of paper. "That is not anything that the public is aware of. I only have it because I called in a favor. You might want to read that over before you see her again."

It was her transcript from when she woke in the hospital. And it was chilling to say the least. But he noticed that she didn't mention the wolf and had told the police that she had no idea what had happened to her to have the scars on her body. They would have hurt, he would imagine. And the fact that she was just a child, a human child, Hunter thought she would have been scared out of her mind. They had made a conclusion that it was more than likely branches from the surrounding trees.

He read how her stepmother, Eva Morris, had been abusive toward her for years. The police had also noted that they'd gone to the home and found the cages that the child had claimed to have slept in. They'd also found the body of Mr. Morris, Slone's father, hidden in the freezer. There was a suicide note on the body that stated that he could not live without his daughter. That in and of itself was very telling.

The SUV that had been found at the scene told a story that was both chilling and heartbreaking. In her transcript, Slone had told them how she'd been locked in the cage in the back and that Eva had had her hair done. The stain of urine had confirmed Slone's story that she'd wet herself. The officer taking the story down had written how ashamed the child had seemed. And upset. He'd also mentioned how Slone told that she'd have to wear the pants to school for several days afterwards. Or so she thought.

Then there was the house. A few weeks after the murder, Slone had walked them through the house. She'd showed them where she'd stashed food and the places she'd be held in the event her stepmother had wanted some quiet time. Even now, all these years after the fact, Hunter wondered how she had survived at all, much less the incident at the river.

"Hunter?" He looked to his right and stared at Luke as he smiled. "You were gone for a long time there, buddy. You okay?"

"I was thinking about the report." Luke had read it as well and he nodded. "What do you suppose a person would be thinking when they do things like this to a child? I mean, I understand that she wasn't hers, but she was only a little girl. And one by all accounts who had tried her best to be someone she could love. I don't understand it."

"I doubt anyone does. And I would even say that neither did Eva. She was greedy and when she found out that marrying Slone's dad was going to get her nothing, she went to the next step, a very violent and horrible step to ensure that she got what she felt she deserved." They both looked down the table when their dad laughed. "She is so traumatized by this, Hunter. I wonder if she will ever recover."

"She will. I think she will with our help. And I think she forgets to be afraid just a little when she's fighting with me." Hunter winked at Luke. "I'm going to make it my life's work to keep her on her toes."

Luke told him good luck. And Hunter was pretty sure he was going to need it. As dinner progressed, the laughter became louder and the ties were loosened. Hunter kept an eye on Slone and enjoyed watching her talk with his dad. Every time she looked like she was pulling away, he'd reel her back in with a joke or a laugh. And he told her over and over how much he enjoyed the scones. When the plates were cleared away, she finally looked at him.

"I would like a word, please." He nodded and stood up. She was pushing back her chair when he moved behind her to pull it out for her. She looked up at him, and he could see the panic in her eyes.

"I'm only being polite, love." She nodded and he helped her to stand. When she moved toward what looked to him like another part of the restaurant, he put out his arm for her. She laid her hand on his and he noticed that she was trembling. Hunter didn't want her to be afraid of him.

"Did I tell you what I do for a living? Well, I used to. When we moved here I became the Alpha. Not that I don't think I'm going to enjoy it, but it wasn't my first choice." She stopped moving and stared at him. "I own the construction company with my brothers, yes, but I also work it, too. I'm more often than not on site when they are."

"Why?" He opened the door in front of them and escorted her in before he answered. What he wanted to do was press her against the wall and take her again, or at the very least kiss her senseless, but he took her to one of the chairs and let her sit.

"Why do I work my company?" She nodded. "I started out working for Dad. And I really enjoy working out of doors more than I do inside. Then there is the added bonus of seeing my projects come to life and become something lasting."

"It's why I grow my own vegetables." When she flushed, he asked her what she grew. "Everything. I wasn't very good at it at first. Most of the time, things failed more than they produced, but I got some books and read online how to do it and it got to be easier. And I've been playing with some of the ways to grow things. It keeps me alive."

"And meat, what do you do about red meat? I'm assuming you don't hunt on your land." She shook her head. "You have things shipped in, don't you?"

"I do. William will bring me what I need monthly. I have large freezers that I keep stocked during the winter months. He can't come in through the water then." Hunter nodded. He'd wondered how she got things to her. "Sometimes he brings the boys — my stepbrothers, I guess — but they're older now and I don't see them very much."

"You need to get out more." He hadn't meant to break the mood, but she got up to pace. He noticed that she did that when she was nervous or had to work something out. He watched the way her pants fit her body with each step, the way her blouse seemed to cup her every curve. He tried to adjust his cock without her seeing, but she turned just as he did. She stared at him until he had to say something.

"I want you." She shook her head. "I'm sorry I hurt you so badly, but I only meant to mark you, not take you like that."

"Why did you? I mean, you saw what I looked like. Why did you even want to...is it just a man thing? Where any woman would do so long as there's some need?" She started pacing again. "I'm not saying I didn't enjoy it, but I don't understand why you'd even want to look at me."

Anger surged up from his heart. He stood up and pulled her into his arms. He held her to him until she stopped struggling. When she did, he lifted her chin up to look into her tear-stained face.

"Who did this to you? Your stepmother? She was jealous of you. You have to know that." She shook her head. "Then who made you feel that you were less than perfection?"

~~~

Slone wanted to curl into his arms and stay there. He was big and warm, his body perfect for holding, but he was going to make her do things she didn't want to do. Maybe, she thought, if she told him the truth, he'd simply walk away. Or at least she hoped he would.

"I was sixteen and he wanted to take me out. I'd never dated before. The press was constantly trying to get me to tell them what I had done to help Eva kill my dad. Or what I had really done to her to make her end up at the bottom of that ravine. So I stayed by myself. But this boy...he was nice to me." She pulled away to stand near the window that looked out over the darkened parking lot. She noticed that the limo was gone and wondered if the other men had left them there. "He took me to dinner. Not anything fancy, but it was nice. I'd had hamburgers before, of course, but I was so excited I think I could have eaten dirt and been thrilled. Then we went for a drive."

"What was his name?" Slone didn't bother looking at Hunter as she thought of that night long ago. She didn't answer him either.

"I was supposed to be home by eleven and it was only just after eight. Early night, I suppose, compared to what dates are now, I guess, but he'd never given me any indication that he was...that he had a plan." Slone ran her fingers down the glass as she continued. "He asked me for a kiss. I'd, of course, never been kissed either so I nodded. I guess I was too eager. I nearly attacked him to get it started. Then he grabbed my breast and twisted it. I pulled back and cringed near the door while he started to unbutton his fly.

"'Come here and suck me off,' he said to me. 'Come here and take my cock into your mouth so I can come. I'm supposed to fuck you, but that's not going to happen. I'm not fucking animal girl.'

"'What?' He laughed at my question. I had no idea at the time what he'd been talking about and so I asked him.

"'Are you kidding me? Everyone knows that you fucked an animal and that's why you got those bite marks on you. Where else are they, Animal Girl? Show me your tits and let me see if he liked biting them, too.'

"I tried to get away, but he grabbed me by the hair from behind. The more I struggled to get away, the more he hit my head against a window. I was passing out when I heard a scream...."

When someone touched her, she looked at him, not really seeing him. The boy was there instead and she fought hard to get away. Suddenly, her wolf took her and she snarled at the man in front of her.

"Slone, honey, it's me." She tried to focus on him. "Slone, you're fine. The boy is gone and I'm here. I'm not going to hurt you."

Slone felt her mind let go of the gripping terror and saw where she was. Her wolf moved along her skin like a caress, and she lay down. She looked at Hunter and what she'd done to him. Moving forward slowly, she waited to see if he would hit her.

"You're very strong, aren't you?" He chuckled a little, and she whimpered. "I'm fine, honey, just fine. I should have known better than to touch you when you were so far away. Come here and lick my wounds closed for me."

She whimpered again and stood very still as he put out his hand. She was sure he thought she was going to snap it off, but he rubbed his fingers through her fur and she moved closer to him. Licking the wounds, she could taste his hot blood and nuzzled deep into his throat. He growled low. Slone started to pull away, but he held her.

"Don't. Not yet. Let me hold you." She moved closer to him, and he held her. "I want to find that kid and tear his nuts off and feed them to him."

He's dead. She pulled back to look at him and he grinned. *I can talk to you this way. How is that possible? I've never been able to do that before.*

"My blood, I guess." She had a feeling he'd done that on purpose, having her seal up the wounds. "I have to admit, I'm glad. I wanted to tell you how beautiful you are as a wolf."

I need to get back to my hotel. He nodded and stared at her. *I don't know how to do that. I have nothing to wear.*

"I don't mind." She growled at him, and he laughed. "All I've thought about since I left you today was how delicious you tasted and how you screamed out my name when I ate you. Do you have any idea how hard I've been since I was inside of you? How much I'd like to be there again? And I want to taste your nipples, pull them into my mouth and suckle them until you come. Are they pink, Slone? Are your nipples thick and long, or are they tiny and just the right size for me to feast on?"

You shouldn't be talking like this. She backed from him, and he moved toward her on his hands and knees. *What are you going to do?*

"Shift." He shifted in mid-step. His wolf moved along his skin like a blanket covering him. And when he was before her in his full wolf, she felt her own start to respond to him. *I want you now. Come here.*

She didn't want to, but her wolf did. As she moved her body along his, she felt a connection forming that she knew was more than alpha to bitch. He was her equal, in more ways than one.

His bite at her shoulder had her snarl at him, and he growled again. When he moved behind her, never letting go of her, she tried to get away.

Not here. I want you to fight me outside, but we have to play nice in here. Christ, I can smell you. You're so heated right now that I could drink from you for hours and never get enough. He mounted her, and she raised her hips up for him. As soon as he filled her, she growled and he took her to the floor.

It was fast, this coupling. He moved in and out of her with hard, pounding strokes. When he sank his teeth into her again, she pushed back against him, needing some relief as well. Hunter never stopped, never slowed until he threw back his head and howled his release. Slone felt each splash of his cum as he filled her. Then he pulled from her and stood back. She turned to look at him.

Shift. She shook her head, and he snapped his canines at her. *Shift, damn it, now. He wants to taste you.*

She let her wolf go and stood up. When he moved toward her, his big wolf licking his lips, she started to back away, but he told her to stop. As soon as she did, he lunged at her, knocking her back against the table.

Slone started to move, but he moved his massive head between her thighs and she felt her juices pour from her body. His tongue made a path from her knees to her inner thigh as he watched her. Opening her legs for him, he seemed to purr at her, and she let them fall open. As soon as his muzzle touched her pussy, she cried out in pleasure.

Come for him, Slone. Let him taste himself on you. He needs his taste of your human so that he can be satisfied. Nodding, she sat up to watch him as he licked her again, this time so close to her pussy she nearly begged him to take her. His tongue entered her, lapped at her so deeply she curled her fingers into his fur and held him there.

She came four times in quick, hard releases. When he stepped back from her, she could see her juices as they covered his fur. Then Hunter was standing before her, and he fisted his cock as he smiled at her.

"You're mine." She shook her head, and he grinned again. "Oh, but you are. I've marked you, and my wolf has as well. And when I take you now, you're going to mark me. Will you bite me, Slone? Make me your mate?"

His cock was thick and the tip purple with blood. There were droplets coming from the tiny hole and all she could think about was taking him into her mouth. When she reached for him, pulled him to where with her fingers could run up and down him, he guided her to her pussy and slid in and out.

"Please." He shook his head, and she knew what he wanted. He wanted her to do something she swore she'd never do. But he moved deeper within her, and her body seemed to pull him deeper.

"Say it, Slone. Say the words and I'll take you." She nodded. "No, you have to say them. Tell me you want me."

"I want you. I need you." He slammed forward, taking her breath away. When he pulled back to nearly the tip and took her again, she wrapped her ankles around him and pulled his mouth to hers. She felt his tongue move along her shoulder even as she felt her climax coming to the edge. When she came, this time so powerfully that she screamed, he commanded her to bite, and she sank her teeth into his shoulder and screamed around him again. The connection was complete, the bond irrevocably tied, and she knew that he'd never leave her now. She slipped into unconsciousness just as he bit her, too.

Chapter 6

Hunter watched her sleep. Getting her into the big bed had been a little tricky, but he was glad that he'd called his dad and not one of his brothers for help. He'd met him at the door with a large duffle bag, and while he dressed first, he wondered just how he was going to get her home. His dad knocked when Hunter was just pulling his shirt over his head. He'd already stuffed their ruined clothes into the bag. The only thing left in it was another one of his shirts.

"Didn't know what to bring her, as I have never been in her room. But I've made some arrangements with the hotel to have them unlock her room when we get there. Said she'd had a little too much to drink." Hunter picked her up into his arms and looked at his dad. "She take you?"

"Yes. And she's not going to her room. I want her in mine." His dad nodded and moved to the door. The ride to the hotel felt like it took fifty years. "She's my mate. She claimed me."

"I can see that." Hunter nodded but said nothing more. "I was talking to that Shawn fella, and you know that she owns that restaurant? And a lot of other things, too. He said when a wolf or other para comes to him with an idea, he sends it on to her. If she likes it, she funds things to help them out and they pay her back not by money, though he said that restaurant could make her a fortune, but in 'pay it forwards,' she calls them. Once she takes on a project or an idea, the person she helps has to help five other people. I guess most of the time, they help out more. Like her lawyer."

"He's human." His dad nodded. "Someone helped him and she ended up with him as a lawyer then."

"Nope. He saved her from being raped as a teenager. Some dick shit was going to take her so he could brag to the others how he'd had…well, kids hadn't been nice to our young Slone."

"Animal Girl." His dad nodded and smiled. "Shawn, he killed the boy then. She told me about the incident, at least that he was dead, but I assumed she'd done it. How did he not end up in prison for the murder?"

"Self-defense. He said that she'd told the officer the entire story, and that if not for his help, she'd be dead. Happened to be a wolf, too, or it might not have worked." His dad looked at the bundle in his arms. "She can't have children, did you know that?"

"She said she couldn't. But I could care less. I need her." His dad had nodded, and Hunter looked down at her. "I never thought of how much a woman could change you until tonight. Or make you feel so…well, so useless and powerful at the same time. She could ask me about anything and I'd give it to her."

"The way it should be."

The hotel had helped him to her floor because they would not put her anywhere else. The manager had explained that Miss Morris was a very welcomed guest there, and though they'd never seen her before, she used their hotel for many meetings and parties. It would not do for her to be put elsewhere she did not want to go. And that was why Hunter was in her suite and not his own.

"You're thinking very hard." Hunter looked at her when she spoke. "Are you changing your mind? You can, you know. No one but you and I know what happened in that room."

"My dad does, and I'm pretty sure he's taken out an ad in every paper in the world by now." He lay down beside her, careful not to get under the covers. They'd never talk if he did. "How are you this morning? I didn't mean to hurt you again."

"I don't hurt." She rolled to her back and looked up at the canopy over the bed. "You don't have to go through with our being together. In fact, I'd be happy to let you out of this. It can't be good for you, this being mated to me."

"Why do you think that? And for the record, I'm thrilled to death to be with you. You're amazing, and you can fuck like nobody's business." She turned to him and looked so sad that he pulled her into his arms. "I'm very happy you're my mate. I know you have a lot of concerns and questions. So do I, but we'll work them out."

"I'm not very good around people." He laughed and she hit him. "I'm serious. It's why I don't go to pack meetings. I keep thinking that I'm going to be found out and then they'll want something from me. A story or some nugget of truth that they think I'm keeping from them."

"As I said, we'll figure it out. We'll do this slowly if we have to. Moving from point one to point two as slowly as you need. But we do need to talk about your fortress. What would you like to do about it and me? I have to be able to come and go, and you need to be there."

"You mean you're not going to make me move out?" He frowned and shook his head. "William said that someday someone would find me and make me...he seemed to think that finding a mate was inevitable and that once he found me, I'd have to follow his rules and I'd do it or be beaten."

"What a dick." She laughed and he did as well. "I'm from this century. I don't know which one he was born into...shit, I have to ask. Did this work with his mate? Did she follow his every rule?"

"Yes. I don't think he ever beat her, but he did lay down the law a great deal. Even his sons used to treat me with a little less respect than they did other males. I think it's...I believed it was a male wolf thing."

"My mother would have had my father pinned to the wall if he'd tried laying down any law to her. She was tough and could be a little on the mean side at times. Not to us but to people she felt were not treating others right. Especially when it came to her family. Mom was way protective of us." Hunter smiled at a memory. "There was this teacher in school. It was a human school, as they hadn't opened a pack one up yet. He said that I couldn't play football because I was too big. That I'd hurt the other children."

"That's just stupid. The sport is rough and if you're small, you can get the shit knocked out of you before the first down." He looked at her, hoping what she was saying was true. "Yeah, I love the game. Leave me alone during football season and we'll get along just fine."

"A woman after my heart." He kissed her nose. "Now if you have season tickets in a nice warm owner's box, we might have a match made in heaven." When she didn't answer him, he looked at her. This was simply too wonderful to be true if she did really have tickets to use.

"I do. I own two teams, as a matter of fact. I've never used the seats, but I have them. I think that some of the staff at the firm uses them, and occasionally they'll use them as a gift in some charity thing, but you can go if you want." He stood up and danced around the room. When she sat up on the bed, holding the sheet to her breast, he stopped and looked at her.

"You're lovely. More than that, you're simply beautiful." He moved toward her when he heard her belly growl. "But I guess I should feed you. How about a nice huge breakfast, then we head back home? We have things to do and people to kick out of your box."

He ordered nearly everything on the menu while she showered. He wanted to join her, but when she winced when she stood up, he decided she needed time to rest. His wolf didn't think so right now, but he calmed him by telling the poor boy that she belonged to them, and he seemed to be okay with it. When she came out of the bathroom, he was beginning to have his own doubts as to whether they should wait until she hurt less.

"I'm hurting." He nodded and got down on his knees to help her pull her shoes on. She stared at him for several seconds before she spoke. "My stepmother was so good to me and Dad when she first started dating him. I'm not comparing you to her, but I need to...I'd like to tell you something."

"You can tell me anything, and I'm glad you don't think I'm like her." She nodded and looked at the window. He noticed that she did that when she was nervous, too. Didn't look the person in the face. He was sure because she was afraid of what she might see there.

"She was really nice to us. She came over when Dad was home and cooked us dinner. Dad wasn't a great cook, and we had someone who lived with us, which was good. But she would make mealtime fun. I even began to think of calling her 'mom.' Then after they were married, almost the same day, she started treating me horribly. She fired Mrs. Pope and told Dad that she was going to do all the work. But she'd have people come in right before he'd get home from a trip and clean up the house." Slone looked at him. "I would be locked in a cage when I was there. School was the only time I was ever free. I had to keep my room clean, which was all right, but she would come in and inspect it every chance she got. Sometimes she'd punish me for something that wasn't right by locking me in my cage for days without food. It's why I have to have so much stock, I think."

"You were so abused, baby. I'm so sorry for that." She nodded and stood up when someone knocked on the door. He didn't check to see who it was and was knocked back when a man shoved his way in. The camera going off was the only thing he heard until she started screaming. He needed to protect his mate, and he shifted.

~~~

Cash kept glancing at the bedroom door and wondering what the hell he could do to fix this. Not only was his child hurt, but his mate had been as well. The officer in front of him looked like he was ready to piss his pants, and Cash was glad now that he'd called Luke in when he heard the screams.

"So what you're telling me is that it was well within his rights as a newspaper man to barge into the honeymoon suite of my brother and his wife. And that you're not going to do shit about it." The officer opened his mouth, and Luke took a step toward him. "If you tell me again that my brother shouldn't have opened the door to him, I will personally hunt down this supposed giant dog and have him eat you for lunch. Where the hell is this thing anyway? Are the other patrons of this hotel safe from him?"

"We're doing a door-to-door search now, sir." Cash had to laugh. And they'd never find him either so far as a dog was concerned. But the big bad wolf might be another story. The newspaper man was being loaded onto a gurney with his hand wrapped up. The camera had been completely destroyed, it seemed.

After they left with the man, Cash knocked on the door. When it opened just a little, he said it was Dad and was let inside. Cash could hear someone throwing up in the bathroom. He looked at Hunter.

"She's sick. I've ordered her something light to eat." Hunter looked at the bathroom door. "I didn't know that man was coming in. Christ, he just barged in like he owned the place. And my wolf only thought to keep her safe."

"That's the way of our beasts. But you don't have to worry about any of them shots getting out. When I got here, I took out the card that had the pictures on it, then destroyed the camera, too. I had a grand old time at it, too, if you want to know the truth. He'll think twice about going somewhere he's not welcome again." They both turned to the door when it opened. "How you doing, darlin'?"

"He hurt you." She moved toward Hunter, and Cash stepped back. She was not just hurting from this, but she looked like she might just be close to losing it. "I knew that things were going too nice for me. I should have just stayed home and none of you would have been involved."

"Yeah, that's not going to get us anywhere, you thinking like that. Luke is handling things right now. He might not be a big time lawyer like you got on your payroll, but that Shawn is letting him run the show. Nearly scared the piss right out of the first cop on the scene." Slone nodded and sat down. Cash sat across from her. "I have to tell you what's going on, honey. Can you take a little more right now?"

"I'm not going to break." He nodded and had to hold back his laughter. "And you should know that when you try not to laugh like you are right now, your cheeks get all red and you look like you're about to bust. Say it and let me go home."

"All right then. You're married." She looked at him, then at Hunter. "We told the police that you were here on your honeymoon and that he barged in on you and Hunter. As of right now, no one knows who you are but Mrs. Emerson."

"I'm not." Cash nodded. "No, I'm not. I mean, I understand why you did it, but won't he be able to go and look for a record of my marriage? And when he doesn't find anything, it's going to make him work twice as hard to get to me."

"It's been taken care of." She stood up to pace. "When I told Shawn what we had to do, he told me he'd call in a few favors. Within ten minutes, there was a record of you and Hunter being married at the justice of the peace here in town last night. The dinner we had was in celebration. Shawn is planning a press conference today. And he's notified the Giles to let them know as well."

"What will that solve?" He started to answer but someone knocked on the door. He waited while Hunter went to the door. Slone sat back down on the bed. "You know this won't work. He's going to realize what a problem it is being with me and he'll want out."

"I doubt that very much. And I think you know it. Nothing is so bad that we can't fix it. And if it ever is, then we work around it. You're going to be all right, Slone. We're family now." She nodded and stood when Hunter closed the door. He didn't look happy.

"There are nine news vans outside the hotel. And the street is being filled with people wanting to get a look at the heiress. They know we're married and want to see you." She shook her head, and Hunter pulled her into his arms. "Then we go with plan B. It's not all that good of a plan, but Graham and Lee think it will work."

"Why don't you go on back home and I'll wait them out? I've done it before. I holed up at a hotel once for nine weeks. I'll be fine." Hunter kissed her and smiled. "You're not going to leave without me, are you?"

"Nope. And you should get any notions of letting me leave you permanently out of your pretty little head. I've grown quite fond of you." She snorted. "Yeah, I know you only want me for the sex, but we're a little crunched for time right now."

Cash couldn't help it, he burst out laughing. It wasn't what Hunter said but the complete and utter shock on Slone's face. He thought for the rest of his days, he'd think of that look and laugh again.

"What do you have planned? And so you know, this is not the end of this conversation. I am not a pushover no matter what I look like right now." Hunter laughed, and she glared. Cash was thinking how much he was going to enjoy watching these two work it out and wondered if they'd let him live with them. Might keep him young just watching them.

"We go out the front door." She looked at Hunter like he'd lost his mind. Cash was beginning to think that when he'd been thrown against the wall, he might have banged his head a little too hard, too. "Wait and listen. They have no idea what we look like, right? As far as you're concerned, no one has seen a picture of you since you were a kid. And trust me, honey, you've changed a great deal since then."

"I don't like you right now." Hunter kissed her again, and she flushed. "I'm trying to be upset with you. Stop kissing me like I'm five."

"You're too beautiful to be five, and what I want to do to you right now requires that you're the age you are." Cash turned away when Hunter pulled her into his arms for a passionate kiss. The boy was besotted with his mate, and Cash loved it. But there were limits on what a father could take. Clearing his throat to remind them he was still there, he waited until Hunter laughed.

"When do you want to do this thing?" Hunter said now and Cash turned. "They're expecting a news conference. Won't her not being here put a crimp in that?"

"I don't care." Hunter was shoving things into a bag as he spoke. "They can all go straight to hell for all I care. Right now, I just want to pack up and go back home. I miss home and the quietness of it."

"It won't be once it gets out where I live." Slone started picking up things, too, and Cash reached for his other sons and told them to start packing, they had ten minutes tops. "And that fence I have around my house will only keep them out for so long before they start to look for ways to get to me."

"And we'll keep them out with our own sort of patrols. There are any number of wolves that will protect you like I would. I figured that out the first week we got there." Hunter turned to him. "What did that lady at the diner tell you when you arrived?"

"She told me that if I was there to see their provider, we should just mosey on down the road and leave them alone. She said that they protected their own." Not exactly what she'd said. She'd told him to get the fuck out of town if he was there only to try and breach the fence. She'd told him lesser men had tried and they had a plot of graves of them in the back of the trash dump. Cash had nearly left that afternoon.

"Mable Carlyle. She needed a startup to open the diner. She said that she wanted to support her kids in a manner she had never had. She didn't have any children. I found out right before I turned her down for lying that she meant the children she supports that are going hungry. She feeds thirty children breakfast before school every day." Cash stopped packing and looked at Slone when she spoke. "She paid me back."

"How much do you still support her with weekly to help pay for those free breakfasts?" She flushed, and Cash didn't think she was going to answer Hunter. He said her name again, and she turned and glared at him.

"I make sure that her cupboards are not empty. Who wouldn't do that for what she does?" Hunter told her not many. "But I can do it, so I do. And it doesn't hurt me even a little. She does a great deal for the people in that town. And if you have even the slightest bit of trouble with that then you can go straight to hell." Hunter only kissed her again.

"How much are you worth?" Cash hadn't meant to ask her, but he just spilled it out before he could think how rude it was. "I know the papers estimated your mother's fortune to be around thirty-four million, but I have a feeling you've done a little better with it. And if these things I've been hearing about you are even half true, I'd say you're worth double if not more."

"Yes on the more part. A good deal better than double as a matter of fact." She shoved the case into his hand and stared him right in the eyes. Cash knew this was going to be epic. "I have just over nine hundred billion. That's not counting what I have invested in smaller companies that are just starting out. I don't know how much that is right now."

"But I bet you have a pretty close estimate." She nodded, then looked at Hunter. He was staring at her like he'd never seen her before. Cash wanted to go to him and shut his mouth, but he had to deal with this on his own, he thought. "You trade on your own, make your own decisions as well, don't you, darlin'?"

"I do. I have Shawn to keep me straight, but he's more of a front man than anything. I also…there are times when he keeps me out of jail. I've been close a couple of times." Cash asked her how, stalling so that Hunter could get a grip. "When a company I've invested in fails, and a lot of them do, I take over and sometimes I make it work. The person who might have been working toward the end that I achieve, he might get a little mad at me."

"You're not kidding, are you?" They both turned to Hunter. "I knew that you had money. A great deal of it, but you're not kidding when you say you're worth billions, nearly a trillion dollars."

"No. Why would I kid about that?" Hunter dropped the case he'd been holding and came toward her. Cash wasn't sure what his plan was, but he looked a little intense. When he pulled Slone into his arms and kissed her hard on the mouth, Cash let out the breath he was holding.

"Do you have a home in every country?" She nodded. "Good. Then you can take me on a honeymoon to see the world. I've never been out of the United States. And you can buy me an engagement ring, too. I can think of any number of things you can buy me right now but, as your husband, we'll go slowly. I think...what if we take a long trip and never come back?"

"All right." Hunter kissed her again and pulled her to the door. "Are we going now? I mean home? I don't have all my things packed up and you haven't even started."

"We are leaving now. I want to get you home as well. And this stuff can be sent to us." Hunter looked at him. "Dad, are you coming? Or are you staying for the press conference?"

He dropped the bag. "Wouldn't miss this for the world."

Chapter 7

Slone wasn't sure what to do with people in her house. She tried to keep away from all of Hunter's brothers who had showed up about an hour after they'd gotten there, but they were all so big and too friendly, too. Slone felt like she simply could not breathe. She wanted them all gone yesterday. When she heard the helicopter coming, she ran outside like it was going to take her away. She felt rather than heard someone come out behind her.

"You expecting that?" She nodded at Ellis, the quietest of all the Emerson men. "I would say by the size of it you're getting a nice supply of something. Do they normally bring things to you this way?"

"I've never had anything delivered before, but I really wanted this. It's a tractor for my garden. I wanted to bring it back on the plane with us, but Hunter didn't want to wait. I guess he was right, but I really wanted to bring this soon. Shawn made the arrangements to have it airlifted to me." Ellis stood next to her. "Have you ever driven a tractor?"

"No. Have you?" She shook her head. "If I asked you to go over there by the shed, would you? I know this sounds kind of stupid and all, but I keep thinking of the Trojan horse."

She laughed when she looked at him. His smile told her he was being serious. Nodding, she moved to the building that would shield her from the large field that was going to be the expansion of her garden effort in the spring. When the large crate was set on the ground, the long chains that held it dropped a few minutes later. As the helicopter moved back into the sky, she came to see the box. The others had come out to join them. Hunter had a crowbar.

"I thought you'd get this tomorrow." The first board came off and she felt her excitement start to rise. Hunter and the others took all the crate boards off and she just stared at her new toy. She wanted to climb up on it and till until all her land was turned over. She knew that she couldn't. First of all, she had only read how to use it and she knew from experience that reading about how to do something and actually doing it were two different things entirely. Instead, she took the large notebook when it was handed to her and grinned. Hunter smiled at her.

"You should see your face right now. You look like a kid at Christmas. Most men would have that look, not a woman, I'm betting." She told him she wasn't most women. "Oh, you got that right. When can we expect the first seed to go into the ground, madam farmer? This year yet?"

"No. I'll have to wait until next year now. I didn't decide to get this until a couple of weeks ago. I have dreamed of having one but didn't want to buy it sight unseen." She wanted to climb up in the seat so bad she could taste it. And when Hunter suddenly lifted her up and sat her on it, she squealed. But she gripped the steering wheel tightly. "This is going to make gardening so much easier for me. And I can do so much more with this that I couldn't before."

"For us." She ignored Hunter's statement for now. They hadn't talked when they returned this morning, and she kept waiting for him to tell her he'd thought it over it and he couldn't handle it. She was waiting for it every minute, and she was pretty sure Cash knew it. The others wandered away as she continued to sit there as Hunter watched her.

"You ready to tell me?" She looked at him, confused. "You've been wanting to tell me something for the past few hours. I've been really patient, but I think that now that we're alone and you have your new toy, you should just tell me."

"You're going to leave me." He didn't say anything, and she continued. "I know it's a lot to take on. And the fact that you saw that I was home safe was really sweet of you, but you don't have to pretend that you want this kind of life. It's not anything I'd wish on anyone."

"And what kind of life do you think you're going to give me? Are you thinking that because a few cameras are going to go off in my face that I'm going to run and hide? Do you really think...well, that's not really a question, is it? You do expect me to hurt you like others have in your life and leave you. I'm not going to. Do you want to know why?" She nodded, and he pulled her down off the tractor. When he went to one knee, she started to back away, but he took her hand. "No, don't leave me. I wanted to tell you this yesterday. After dinner. But you distracted me. Then the cameras and my dad. But I wanted...no. I needed to tell you that I love you. I know you think it's not possible, but I do. And I want you to marry me for real."

"You don't have to do this." He nodded and slipped the ring over her knuckles. "You really...I thought I was going to give you a ring."

"This one was my mother's. My dad brought it to New York with us and gave it to me right before we met you at the restaurant. I wanted so desperately to ask you then, but as I said, you distracted me." She started to pull her hand free to look at the ring, but he held her. "I'm in love with you, Slone. I think that I've waited for you all my life, and when you stood up to me that first time and every time after, all I could think about was you were my mate, my equal in all things. I know that I've been a pain in the ass and if you don't believe me right now, I can understand. I didn't exactly move with my best foot forward where you're concerned."

"People aren't going to leave us alone. I don't even know if I can be what you need in a mate. I'm terrified of being hurt again." He stood up and pulled her into his arms and held her. "What about you being the Alpha? The pack is going to expect me to be there standing next to you. I don't know if I can do that." She wanted to pull from him and run for being such a failure to him. "I'm not going to simply get over this because you want me to. I don't know if I ever will."

"Then we work around it. And most of the people in our pack already know that you're very private. Hell, most of them have warned us off from you the first time we asked them about you. They know that you're there for them if they need you. And I have a feeling that most of them will come to you, however necessary, to get anything they need. You've been their alpha long before I took you as my mate."

She didn't know if she could do any of the things he was going to need her to do. But she also knew that if anyone could make her do it, it would be him. Slone looked up into his eyes. She could see his love for her and his understanding. But would it be enough?

"You just want my box seats at the opera." He looked at her, wide eyed. "You can't be serious. You like the opera, too?"

"Yes. It's a passion of mine." She didn't know if he was kidding or not and continued to stare at him. "When I was small, about eight, my mom took me and Luke to the opera. She had won four tickets to it from some contest. I don't remember. Anyway, they got a sitter and we went. Dad sat beside me and we watched the entire thing, not having a clue what was being said but understanding it completely. Luke fell asleep on Mom's lap, but I talked about it for days."

"Opera and football. Next you'll be telling me that you like gardening." He shuddered and shook his head. "Well, I guess I have one thing I can do on my own."

"Can I move in here with you?" She looked at the house and tried to imagine him being there all the time. "And so you know, Dad wants to live here as well. Not my brothers. They want to live in the building that they're working on. I thought we'd make that the pack house. But I want to learn about you, and living with you is the best way. Besides, I want to make love to you every chance I get."

"I don't know how this will work. I might...I know that I'm going to take some getting used to this." He nodded and held her hand as they walked to the house. "What if it doesn't work? What if you find out that I'm a raving lunatic and you can't stand it?"

"Then we'll figure something out. Don't look for trouble that's not there. I do enough of that on my own. Maybe you can be the sane one and I can be the idiot. I've been that where you're concerned. We can do this, just keep telling yourself that." She didn't know if he was right or not, but she supposed that she could always simply give him the house and move away again. She'd done it before. When they entered the house, Luke was on his cell phone and he didn't look happy. When he hung up, he sat them both down.

"The story hit the paper this morning. I had no idea and not sure what I could have done to stop it by the time I might have.... Never mind. There's a seven-page spread about you, Slone. Not only have they brought up the incident at the river, but also the speculation as to your marriage to some low life." Luke looked at Hunter. "Couldn't really dispute that one, because to do so would have required your name. So for now, you're a low life."

"I can live with that." Hunter got up and started to brew tea. Slone looked at Luke when he took her hand into his. She felt so comforted by it she nearly cried. "Leave my woman alone, shit head, and tell us the rest." She nearly jerked her hands away when Hunter laughed.

"He's kidding. Anyway, there is speculation that you're married and no one knows to who, but that's not going to be a concern. Shawn said that the paperwork is filed and complete. The story on your childhood is old news, but you said you expected that. What I'd like to propose, and you can say no if you want, is that you set up a meeting and let the press in to ask their questions."

She stood up so fast that she knocked the chair back. He couldn't be serious. As she moved out of the room, she heard him calling for her to come back but was terrified beyond reason. When she came to a door she couldn't open she looked behind her and saw Hunter there. He held the door closed with his hand over her head.

"Take deep breaths before you pass out." She nodded, panicking more. "Listen to me, Slone, you have to breathe or you're going to make yourself sick.

She nodded and tried to control her breathing. Every time she thought of being in front of the people who had never left her alone, she started to panic all over. Finally, he shook her and she started to cry.

"He wants to humiliate me. Put me on show for him and the rest of you." She started to shake and he held her to him. "I don't want to stand there and have them judge me again. They hate me."

Hunter only held her but said nothing. She knew he was thinking she was stupid and nearly told him to leave her. But as she figured he'd be doing that soon enough, she clung to him as tightly as she could. When she pulled back finally, she looked at Luke, who was leaning against the wall.

"You must think I'm an idiot." He shook his head and smiled at her. "In the event you didn't notice, I'm not keen on the idea of being in front of reporters. They've taken their bite out of me a few times over the years."

"Yeah, I got that. But I think you're wrong." He moved into the room with them and sat on the couch. He looked good there and smiled at her as he continued. "Do you know why they hound you? It's because you let them. If you give them what they think they want, then they'd be bored with it and move on to something more."

"I've tried this before." Luke nodded, and she glared. "You knew that before you suggested this. Why did you do that when you knew that it wouldn't work?"

"The reporters were given questions they could ask you and ones that they could not. Of course, they were going to go after you. The list of things that you wouldn't talk about was longer than the things you would. And, of course, that just made them want more. Especially since the questions they needed were just what you should have given them. The why, when, what, and where. You never answered any of those for them."

"They want everything." He nodded. "You think I should give them every detail. How I wet my pants? How she locked me in the basement for days on end with nothing more than the mice to keep me company?"

"I do." She sat down and wondered what Hunter thought of this. When she looked at him, she could see that he agreed with his brother. "I'm not going to let them rip me apart again. You have no idea how long it took me to...I've never gotten over this. How could I?"

"Because this time you have us." She looked at Hunter and saw that he truly believed that would solve it all. "You didn't have anyone before. You were quite literally all alone. But you won't be this time. You have all of us."

There was no way they could be serious. She moved to her office and looked along the walls for the tape. Bringing it back, she slipped it into the player and hit play. The first few seconds of the tape was of a table and a chair. She came into view a few seconds later. Slone left the room to go outside to her garden and left them there.

~~~

Luke watched the interview. They tore her apart. Every little thing she said, they pounced. Even when she'd reached for the glass of water in front of her, one reporter asked her if she was going to kill herself on television. By the time the fifty-minute interview was over, he was so pissed that he wanted to find each and every one of them and murder them in their beds. He looked at Hunter. And he looked like he was making a list right now.

"They destroyed her." Luke nodded. "Christ. Just when I think I can help her, someone else comes along and breaks her down again."

"She's not going to break, and she's not destroyed. Not yet at any rate. This only proves that she needs to get up in front of them and tell them all that happened. If not, they are going to keep at her until she breaks or breaks one of them. And Hunter, you know that if she tries to break one of them, someone will kill her." Hunter gave a short bark of laughter. "She needs to show them that she's not a victim. Right now, they prey on her because she lets them. As soon as they are satisfied that she's not, then they will leave her alone. Every time she closes the door in their face, she simply makes them want to pound harder on it to get it open."

Hunter got up and went to the window. This room like most of the house was open and had plenty of light coming in. Luke could see Slone as she worked in her garden, and wasn't surprised to see Dad out there with her. The two of them didn't appear to be talking, but he would bet that neither of them cared. Luke saw his dad jump back from something and Slone laugh. He wondered what it might have been.

"Dad has always had an unhealthy fear of snakes. I would bet that's what he saw just now." Hunter sounded so down that Luke felt bad for telling him about the paper. "She won't want to do this. I think you're right, but she won't want to do it. Dad might be able to talk her into listening, but she'll have to decide this on her own."

"I think the sooner we do this the better. Before much longer, someone is going to find out that she lives here and the media will hit the town like a tidal wave." Hunter nodded. "The mayor in town, I'm betting at this very moment he's calling them to let them know she's here. And not only that, but inviting them to stay at his house while they try and destroy her. She needs to get on the wagon before he does this."

"I'll talk to her. But I want you to do as much research as you can on what they might ask her. I'm sure that you can't anticipate all of the questions, but it will be a start. And Luke?" Hunter turned just as he stood up to do what he'd asked him to do. "I want you to be just as vicious as you can about them. I don't want her wrapped in cotton when this thing happens."

"I will." Luke pulled the tape out of the player. "I'm taking this for research. Tell her I'll bring it back to her when I'm finished." Hunter nodded but said nothing. He just stood there watching his mate and dad working in the yard.

Luke was going to make this work for her if it was the last thing he ever did. He was nearly to the hotel when he heard from Graham. Things were beginning to heat up.

"I just got a call from that reporter I knew in DC. He wants to sit down with me and ask me about the woman who lives in the gilded cage. I told him I had no idea what he was talking about and hung up." Luke closed his eyes as soon as he parked his truck. "I have a feeling he's not going to be the last one either, is he?"

"I would say you're right." He told him about the newspaper article that was coming out and what he'd proposed for Hunter and Slone to do. "I think this is her best bet to get this over once and for all."

"Yeah, I agree. I have...what if we sort of spread it around town that this thing is coming out. I mean, there isn't a person here that she's not done something for. You think they'd rally behind her and keep her safe until we can get this thing set up?"

Luke thought it was a wonderful idea. "But don't go at it like you're trying to get their support. Sort of do it like you can't believe these people won't give this shit up." Graham said he'd do it. And Luke thought of something else. "The mayor in town, do you think he has any skeletons in his closet that we can use?"

"I'm betting he has a whole house of them, and I know just the person who can tell me. Did you know that Pete has decided to hang around? Said he wanted to see how a real Alpha did his job. I think the man is smitten with Slone." Luke thought he was as well but said nothing. "I'll talk to him first. He might have a way of hitting this thing with the right people in the right way."

Luke had no doubt that he would. As he stood in line to get his messages at the hotel, he noticed that the clerk wouldn't look at him. When he was next, the man looked so terrified that Luke was sure if he said "boo" to him he'd shit himself.

"I'm sorry, sir, but we have to ask you to leave." Luke looked at the two cops that suddenly appeared on either side of him. "We've overbooked and as you and your family have...you had no...." The man looked at the cops.

"No problem." His luggage and that of his brothers hit the floor beside him. "We'll just settle the bill and be on our way."

"There was some damage done to the room and you're going to have to pay for that, too. It was...it was pretty bad, so you know." Luke looked at the cop who spoke, then at the clerk who had backed away. "You should just give us your credit card and we'll tally it up for you."

"I need to contact my brothers first, please. There might be a few things missing from our things and we can't have that." His laptop was dropped beside him, and had it not already been in pieces, it would have been when it hit the floor. Luke reached for Hunter and told him what was going on.

I'm coming. He told him to hurry just as the first punch knocked him back. He got in a few punches of his own, but rather than shifting, he took their abuse. By the time he was being lifted up after being beat to shit, Hunter told him help was on the way. Luke told him it was a mite too late for help.

They're hurting you? Luke said yes. *Christ, I'm coming there. Hopefully before they finish with you. I want to knock a few heads together myself.*

Just meet me at the jail. I'm thinking that's where I'm headed, or the morgue. More than likely the latter of the two. Someone picked him up by his leg and dragged him out of the hotel. *You might want to bring me a change of clothes, too. I'm bleeding all over these.* Luke felt himself slipping away and could still hear Hunter screaming at him as he closed his eyes.

He felt himself being hurdled into a cell what seemed an eternity later. Luke mumbled that he had a lawyer coming and they laughed. Luke hoped Hunter could find him a good one. He had a feeling it was going to be bad before this was finished.

Luke felt like every bone in his body had been cracked. His head was pounding like a jackhammer had replaced his brain, and he couldn't see out of one eye. If he could have shifted, he would have been healed by now, but he was actually afraid that if he did, they'd empty every gun in the place into him. Instead, he just sat there bemoaning his fate.

When someone came down the hall, he could hear the tip-tip of heels before he saw her. Slone looked like a vision. She stood there staring at him for several seconds. He wondered what she was thinking when she spoke. He started to stand and then just fell back. He was too hurt to be polite right now.

"You say this will work. That you'll be right there beside me if I do this?" Luke had to think what she was talking about, then nodded. "You know what it took for me to come down here? Do you have any idea how hard this was for me? But they hurt one of mine and I will not sit still for that. They are going to pay."

"Christ, will you let me help you when you go for blood? And as for you coming down here? I would say really hard. But you look really pretty. I've never been able to turn down a woman in heels, and you look like you were born to them." She snorted. "You do that well, too. Did Hunter show you how?"

"No. And the only thing that took any effort for me was to decide whether or not to bring a gun. Hunter told me not to, but you've no idea how tempted I was to come here with guns blazing." He nodded, not sure where she was going with this, and told her he was glad she'd decided not to shoot him. "Not you, you moron, the asshole that hurt you. I was ready to come here before Shawn arrived but was told to wait."

She dropped to her knees, and he looked at her. She'd been crying, and he reached out and rubbed a tear from her cheek. "Don't cry, honey. I'm going to be fine once I die." He laughed, and she smacked him. The pain wasn't as bad as he let on, but he still moaned. The sound of shouting had them both looking at the door. All he could think of was "Christ."

His dad and all five of his brothers were leading the pack. Shawn and five more men in suits were right behind them. The chief of police was there, as well as one of the officers that had beaten him up. Luke stood up when they stopped in front of his cell.

Shawn turned to look at the cop and drew back and slammed his fist into his face. Luke watched as the man fell over and hit his head on the cell behind him. Then Shawn turned to look at him. Luke thought he could see a little pain in his eyes, but otherwise he looked like he'd enjoyed that.

"I want my client out of this cell and taken to the hospital this minute. And if he gets anything less than excellent care, Miss Giles will own that as well." Luke waited until the door opened before he started to speak. But Slone entered his mind before he could.

Act as if you hurt a great deal more than you do, please. It'd be better for the reporters outside this building. In fact, if you could lean heavily on your dad, it will play better for the six o'clock news. Luke stumbled a little and took his dad's shoulder. *I'm going to do this, but if you get hurt again, I'm going to be really pissed at you.*

Yes, Alpha. She stared at him before she nodded. Luke kissed her cheek and then let her lead him out of the cells. He was surprised when the cop that he'd hit and the one that Shawn hit were put into his cell. Safe keeping, he was told as they moved out and into a throng of people with cameras and microphones.

Chapter 8

"I have a request for a meeting, sir. Her name is Slone Morris." Ben looked at his secretary. He hated the fact that he'd had to hire a male to do the job, but the country being what is was made it difficult for a man, even a married one, to have any fun anymore.

"And that's supposed to blow wind up my skirt why?" Allen Wagner looked confused. "Why should this woman want a meeting with me, and why on earth should I do it?"

Mother fuck, it was getting harder and harder to get a person working for you who could get a fucking joke once in a while. This idiot, his fourth in as many years, was as dumb as a fucking post.

"You don't know who Slone Morris is?" He sounded incredulous, which pissed Ben off. He was Ben K. Conklin, for Christ's sake...the mayor of this little burg that had been voted as having the lowest crime rate every year since he'd taken office. And, of course, he was going to keep it that way even if he had to continue burying the ass-wipes in his backyard.

"As a matter of fact, I don't have a clue. Is she some rock star that wants to come here and hide out while she dries her ass out? Maybe some drug lord that wants to come here for the peace and quiet? Why the fuck don't you just tell me who she is and then I can make an intelligent decision on whether or not I want to see her?"

Wagner laid a file on his desk and stood there waiting. Ben was going to kill this little shit. When he opened the file, there was a cover of one of those "who's the richest" kind of things. He glanced it over before turning to the next page. There he saw the name Morris/Giles. Ben looked up at Wagner.

"This her?" He nodded. "What the hell does she want with me?" Ben continued to look through the papers and every article claimed that she was *the* richest—not just one of the richest—woman in all the world. He found one that reported that she was worth millions, another billions, and a few that stated that her worth was incalculable. Whatever the hell that meant.

"She said she would like to set up a meeting with you as soon as possible. Something about funding and land development. Plus, she would like to set up a meeting with the community as well." Ben went back to one of the articles that said she had invested several million dollars in a land project that gave one small town a revenue of over eighty million over a ten-year period. More than his little town had ever made since someone had plopped the first house in the dirt.

"Make it happen as soon as she can get here." Wagner nodded and started away, and Ben called him back. "Clear my calendar for the entire day and set up a lunch and dinner at that new place on Tenth. We'll show her what we can provide if she wants to come here and help us out."

"She's here, sir." Ben looked at the man, wondering if he could pull out his gun and shoot him right now and if anyone would miss him. "In town, I mean. She said that she arrived some time ago. And she said whenever is convenient for you; she doesn't want to put you out."

"Call her back and tell her that today would be fine. Then I want you to cancel my appointments for the day. Can you do that?" Wagner shook his head, and Ben put his hand on the desk drawer that held his gun. "Why not?"

He was speaking in exasperated politeness and he was pretty sure the effort was being lost on Wagner. "You don't have any appointments for me to cancel."

Ben stood up and Wagner ran out of the room. It was a good thing he had because when Ben sat back down, he was holding his gun. Mother fuck, he needed a break. Taking several deep breaths, he looked at the file again.

It was all there. Her supposed worth, her ability to turn ten cents into ten million almost overnight. She had programs for people coming out of the workforce for any number of reasons, and help to get them working again. Most of her charitable donations were to smaller groups that helped children, victims of crimes, or the children of parents who were victims of crimes that had left the children without bread winners or support. Her donations alone were enough to make his mouth water. To woo and win a woman like this would be amazing.

"Wonder if she has a family?" He laughed at his own joke, thinking how he'd work hard to get the old broad to like him enough to leave him a little something in her will. He wondered just how old she was and was looking for anything on her when he came to the final pages of the file.

"Mother fuckballs." The kid that had her parents killed. It wasn't what the papers said happened, of course. Ben had always been under the opinion that she and the stepmother had killed off dear old Dad, then concocted a scheme to have the daughter go missing, just like it had happened at the first of their plan. Then the kid had gotten greedy, knocked the stepmother over the falls, and collected all by her lonesome. Smart kid, he'd always thought, and now it appeared she'd grown into a smarter woman. And she wasn't old at all. Ben estimated her to be about twenty-eight or so.

"Well, I guess her adopting me is out, but maybe I can convince her that I'm deeply in love with her and have a little turn-about on her. Marriage and death suits me just fine." He looked up when someone knocked on his door. Wagner again.

"Sir, Miss Morris will be here at eleven. She said that she will be bringing a few people with her. She hopes that you don't mind. I already assured her that it would be all right with you." Ben nodded. "Also, she has invited you to dinner, you and a date. She said that you may bring anyone you please."

He looked at the clock. Of all days for him to sleep in, today had to be it. Christ, it was just going on ten now. He had just an hour, less if she was one of those early people, to get cleaned up and ready for her. And to find a date. He looked at Wagner as he stood there.

"Call Marie and ask her if she's free tonight. Tell her who it is we're having dinner with and to dress up nice. Also, see about having my blue suit brought to the cleaners." Wagner was making notes on his little phone. "No time for a haircut, but do have Jimmy come here right now and fix me up."

"Anything else?" There was plenty but nothing he had time for. Ben was almost thinking that she'd planned this but changed his mind. How the hell would she know what time he came in? But he did look at Wagner.

"Did she happen to call in earlier and you told her I wasn't in?" Wagner nodded. "Why would you do that?"

"She asked." He moved out of the room before Ben could fire him. And he would, too. Just as soon as this was over the man was going to be out on his ass. Ten minutes later, Jimmy came in and fussed with his hair for ten minutes before just spritzing some water on it and combing it. And for this, he charged Ben fifty bucks. Another dick on his list of people to get rid of.

She showed up at five till. He had been sitting at his desk practicing how to come to her when Wagner simply showed her in. He'd been in mid-practice, putting his hand out to her and smiling when she arrived. Without missing a beat, she took his hand and sat. The nine people with her stood right behind her chair. To say he was intimidated would have been a gross understatement.

"Miss Morris, how are you? I certainly didn't expect anyone of your caliber to visit me on this fine Tuesday morning." One of the men handed her a tissue, and she held it tightly in her hand. Ben wasn't sure what that was about but wondered if she was wiping his sweat off. He'd been fucking nervous.

"It's Friday, Mayor Conklin, not Tuesday. Perhaps if you had a better work ethic you'd know that." Ben started to stand when she snapped at him to sit. He sat down so hard his teeth snapped together. "Now. The reason I'm here is that I wanted to inform you that I'm having a press conference in four days. You'll be given details on it when we are closer to the event, but I do want you to make accommodations for the press. They will have meals, of course, as well as any electrical equipment they need. Here is a list that I was given by someone who would know the ins and outs of an event this large."

Ben took the paper and saw that it was a staggering amount of things. And expensive. He looked up at her when she continued speaking. He was still trying to figure out why in his town when she said something that had him stiffen.

"I'm sorry. Did you say that you're having it at the high school? What the hell did you—?" She cocked a brow at him, and he felt ten again. "I'm sorry, what the heck do you want to have it there for? I mean, we have a nice-sized conference room just down the hall from here. I can show it to you if you'd like."

"It won't be big enough. There will be people coming from all over the world for this, and I want to accommodate as many of them as I can. I would hope that you'd call school off for the day and have some of the children help out by setting up chairs and concession stands." Another file came his way. "This is a list of the charitable organizations that are within this town and the person in charge of each of them. I'd like for each of them to have a sizeable booth set up in the halls to sell refreshments and food. I will make sure that the press is aware that this is something that I want."

It was on the tip of his tongue to ask her if she got everything she wanted, but he was pretty sure she did. He looked this list over and saw that the school also had a fundraiser to help kids get to camp for the next spring. He wondered how she'd found this information when he'd had no clue. But then he didn't have a bazillion dollars either.

"Miss Morris, perhaps if you gave me some idea what this might be about, then maybe we can work together on it. I do have some knowledge of press conferences." She only sat there tapping her foot. "I would not tell a soul about what it's about."

"You won't because when the rest of the world finds out, you will, too. I have told you all you need to know." She pointed to the man to her left. "This is Luke Emerson, my attorney. You might remember him from the other night when you had your goons arrest him and put him in jail. You might want to tread lightly where he is concerned. I don't think he cares for you overly much."

"I'm not sure...." He tried to remember what he'd done to this man when he remembered the hotel. "I assure you, Miss Morris, that after all the facts were given to me, I realized my mistake immediately. By the time I made my way to the jail, Mr. Emerson had already been released and as he'd left no forwarding address, I had no way of telling him how profoundly sorry I was."

"I bet you are." When she stood up, each man with her seemed to come alive with tension. Ben had never seen men more...he was going to say "intense" but the word he was searching for was "scary." These men were scary. Ben wasn't sure what to do when Luke sat down as she was moving out the door, the men surrounding her.

"You and I have a lot to do and a very short amount of time to do it in." Ben nodded and sat back down. Luke handed him yet another file. "This is a list of people that are to be in the front of the news reporters. There will be no deviating from this list, and if one of them does not wish to appear there, I will give you a name of another person. You will follow these rules."

"And where am I to be when she has her day in the lime light? At the back of the room. Perhaps I can hold her train for her as she moves along with her cape and crown." Ben knew the moment he opened his mouth that it was the wrong thing to say. Luke only stared at him, and Ben felt himself squirm. Nothing a mayor wanted to do when in front of a lawyer.

"You'll be seated with Miss Morris, provided you can keep your mouth shut and not speak until she asks you something." Ben nodded. Christ, he was pissed, but short of telling her she couldn't do this, he was going to have to play ball with her. For now anyway. It was nearly four o'clock when Luke left his office, and Ben felt as if he'd been drained. Who knew that there was so much to a press conference? He supposed his assistants worked much harder than he'd thought. Not that it mattered. He did pay them well enough, he thought.

~~~

Hunter stood outside the bathroom door, his heart twisting every time he heard Slone throw up. He'd been so proud of her. She'd done what she'd needed and no one would have known that she was sick inside with it. When the door opened, he reached for her and helped her sit on the couch.

"I don't ever want to do that again." He didn't say anything to her. They both knew that this was just the beginning. "He is such an asshole. Where on earth was he dug up from?"

"I would say someone just shit him on a rock and the sun hatched him." They both looked up at his dad when he spoke. "How you doing, darlin'? I brought you in a cup of tea and some of your scones."

Slone took the tea but declined the scones. His dad took two off the plate before setting it on the little table. Hunter just shook his head. His dad had been acting as sort of houseboy and best friend since he'd moved into the bedroom on the upper floors. The man was having a great time working in the garden with Slone as well. And yesterday, he'd driven her tractor for the first time and decided he was going to be a farmer.

"Did you know that cows need five acres for two of them, but sheep can have one per? Interesting. I can't decide on which I want to start with. What do you think, son?" Hunter just stared at him. He had no idea what he was talking about. But apparently Slone did.

"There's this farmer that I helped a few years back that raises both. He's on a bigger scale than we can have here, of course, but he might let you come out for a few weeks and see what you can learn from him. He and his family have been farming for a long time." His dad left after she told him she'd set it up for him.

"You do know that he's going to have a herd of both here in a few days, right?" Slone nodded and smiled. "You really like him, don't you?"

"He's the nicest man I know." Hunter tried to look wounded. "Okay, he's one of the nicest men I know. I really like Luke and Ellis, too."

He tickled her until she begged him to stop. Then he picked her up and put her on his lap and held her. She snuggled into his neck and he kissed her head. He loved holding her, and she was getting used to him touching her all the time. In fact, he'd been surprised when she'd hugged him that morning, and had to stand there like an idiot for five minutes just marveling at how wonderful it had felt.

"He's not a nice person." Hunter nodded. "We're going to have to put someone in office soon that can be trusted and will see that the entire town is full of people who need help, not just his buddies."

"I agree. You should run." He laughed when she punched him. "I'm joking, but I have a feeling you might know of someone to put there. It wouldn't be my dad, would it?"

"I asked him, and he said no. I think he's enjoying working around here. I love...he's very kind to me, and he doesn't push me into things. Not that you have, but he's more...I guess he's more gentle at getting me to open up. Yesterday, he had me explaining to him why I save my seeds and reuse them for an hour before I realized I was enjoying myself." Hunter had heard about the seeds and the reusing them from his dad, too. Hunter was surprised at how much Slone's little farm was self-sufficient. And it really did support the household, too.

"He's having a wonderful time as well. And the fact that you and he can do this is good for you both. But the tractor was his crowning glory. I think he'd use it to drive everywhere if you'd let him. I've never seen him so excited about a piece of farm equipment before." She laughed and stretched over his lap. Hunter felt his cock thicken and held her over him when she started to stand.

"You are very...horny, aren't you?" He nodded, not willing to deny himself when she was right there. "You do know that we're in an office and that anyone could walk in on us."

"It's what makes it exciting. The thrill of being caught." He wiggled his brows at her. "Wanna fool around?"

She still had on her skirt, and he ran his hand up under the hem and watched her face. She had on thigh-high stockings, and he moaned when he touched the warm flesh just above them. He turned her around so that she was facing him and had her put her knees on either side of his hips. She couldn't sit down as her skirt was too tight, so he pulled it up and over her hips and groaned at the sight.

"Christ, woman. Where did you get these?" Panties. He knew that was what they were called, but these were nothing more than a little patch of silk with strings. Hunter cupped her bare ass and brought her down on his throbbing cock. "I want to take you like this. Have you ride me while I suckle at your breasts. You get in too much of a hurry for me and I never get my fill of them."

"You are the one that hurries me." She pulled her blouse up and over her head and dropped it on the floor. Her nipples were hard peaks under the pretty white camisole she had on. "I shop online for my clothes. Most of the time, since I wear shorts or lounge pants, I splurge on my underthings. Do you like it?"

He nodded and rolled her hips over his cock. He wanted to take her just like this, but she was right, he did rush them at times. But she was so amazing, and he loved making love to her. When she put her hands on his shoulders and rolled her hips again, he held her tightly against him.

"I want you to ride me." She nodded and continued her slow gait. "That's it, baby. But I want to be inside of you when you do it."

He sat her back on his thighs, and he reached for his belt. She smacked his hands away and pulled his belt off him and dropped it on her blouse. When she reached into his pants and wrapped her hand around him, he rocked upward into her hot palm.

"You're so hard and silky. And I love how you feel when you slide in and out of me. It's the most amazing thing." He nodded and leaned back. She pulled his tie free with her free hand and then did something that had him nearly come in her hand. She ripped his shirt open with buttons flying everywhere. "I can't wait."

"I can see that." When she leaned in and took his nipple into her mouth and bit down, Hunter held her to him. "You're going to be very disappointed in me if you keep this up. I'm going to come before you get your pleasure."

"I love watching you. And it will give me a great deal of pleasure to see you come." He nodded and let her explore him. Every touch of her fingers brought him closer to rolling her over and pounding into her, but he held himself back. This was the most erotic thing he'd ever had done to him. When she sat up, he helped her pull the camisole off and he cupped her bare breast in his hand and brought it to his mouth. She was panting over him faster now, and he still hadn't been freed. Reaching between them, he unsnapped his pants and pulled his zipper down. She had him wrapped in her hand before he could pull his pants down more.

"Let me be inside of you." She nodded, and he lifted her up to pull his pants to his knees. When she came down, he held his cock, and she lowered herself onto him slowly, riding him every inch of the way. "I'm going to come soon. I can hardly hold back now."

"I want to feel you in me as deep as you can go." He pulled her to him, her clit rubbing his groin with each stroke. When she lifted her breast to his mouth, he took as much of her in as he could, then sucked. He had to hold her tighter before she bucked off him.

"Come," he commanded her and captured her scream with his kiss. He knew there were others in the house and if she screamed now, they'd be caught. When he cried out again, he rolled her over and onto her back. She was coming again when he nuzzled her neck.

"Bite me." He licked her pounding pulse as she begged him. "Please, Hunter, bite me and I'll come so hard that you'll feel it, too."

Hunter felt his balls tighten, and he knew that as soon as she tightened around him again with her release he was going to join her. Sinking his teeth into her skin, he tasted blood and something he didn't recognize, but loved the difference. Hunter felt his cock release. He roared around her flesh even as he felt her bite him as well. When she screamed again, he knew that this was a bonding unlike before; this one made them one.

Dropping down over her, he held her to him. His love for this woman was growing more and more daily, and he realized how happy he was. He looked down at her as she slept and knew that no matter what happened with this press conference, good or bad, he'd be content to live behind the gates with her until he died. Hunter closed his eyes and smiled. Christ, he loved his mate.

Chapter 9

"This is what the email will look like." Slone looked at Lee as he sat in front of her. She knew that she should be paying attention, but she didn't want to think about what was going to happen in a few days. He said her name, and she looked out the window.

"Is it right, you think? That I do this, is it the right thing to do?" When he didn't answer her, she looked at him. "You don't, do you?"

"I do. But I'm worried about you. You're terrified and I don't blame you, but I swear to you, none of us will let anyone hurt you. Mentally, physically, or verbally. You're our sister now, and we protect what's ours." She stood up and pulled her tin of scones down and put on water for tea. He got up and started pulling down cups, three she noticed. "Once Dad hears the tin open, he's going to be right here and you know it. How a man can hear that thing opening is beyond me when he can't even hear me when I scream at him about coming in for dinner."

"He has selective hearing." They both laughed. "I'm so glad you guys are staying here. I know that I get a little freaky at times and run away, but I'm happy you're here." He nodded.

"Me too. Luke loves the system you set up for him. I never understood why he never wanted to work with a big firm, but he said he'd not be able to do it for long. I think he's content to simply be there when we need him. He said he never wanted to be that big."

Slone nodded and thought of Luke as the mayor of this town. She'd never talked to Hunter about it or to Luke, but she'd have to soon. He'd do very well at it.

As soon as the tea kettle whistled, she heard the door behind them open. When she turned expecting to see Cash, she was startled to see William.

"What's happened?" He shook his head and sat down. He looked grief-stricken and she just knew that something had happened to his family. "Tell me what I can do for you."

"Don't do this." She stepped back at the anger in his voice. "I'm ordering you as your guardian not to do this press conference. You don't need to tell the world what happened that day. Just…why don't you go on living like you are and just let it go? Things were working so much better for me when you're here, and I think you should keep doing it. What do you care what they think? Huh? You have all the money in the world at your fingertips. Why do you want to do things differently now? After all this time?"

She sat down and stared at him. Slone thought that of all people, he'd be thrilled about this. And he wanted her to stay locked up like this? Slone had come to realize over the past few days that she was getting to like having others around. Not a lot, but a few at a time didn't send her into fits like it had before.

"You have got to be kidding." Slone looked at Ellis, as he sounded angry as well. "Why does this even have anything to do with you? You're not the one holed up here like a caged animal. And I think she's had enough of that. And why should she be listening to you? You can't order her around to do shit. Do you have — ?"

"You have no idea what I've been doing for her all these years. I've been picking up her food and bringing it to her for years. And when she wanted something brought to her, I had to load up my boat and come out here with it. That would take hours out of my day. I've given up a great deal for her." William stood up. "And she wants to bring this up again, now? What about my father? What do you think he'd say about this? Do you think he'd be happy that you're going to have his name brought up, too?"

"I've paid you." William glared at her. "And very well, too. As for you bringing me things, you never had to do that. I have told you over the years that I'd find a company to do it for me, but you insisted."

Before she could say anything more, both Hunter and Cash came into the room. Cash looked ready to do battle, but Hunter stood behind her with his hands on her shoulders. She could feel his support as though he were wrapping her in it.

"You think that's been enough? My God, I've only done this so you'd stay here out of my life." She was stunned at William's confession, but he wasn't finished yet. "I only took you into my home because Dad made me. All those years of you staying with us cost us so much. Because you couldn't be out, we had to cancel trips. If there were more than five people in the house, we had to make sure that you were safely hidden away. There were so many things that we did because of you."

"You crippled her." She started to tell Cash that wasn't it, but he nodded. "You're the reason she's like she is. Had you put forth some effort in getting her help, or even just helping her cope, she might have been a functioning part of a pack rather than what she was when we got here."

"She was a hunted woman." Slone stared at William. "Do you think we wanted her? Christ, my wife and I were just having our own child and we were saddled with her, too. Did you know that she's the sole reason that my dad is dead and not enjoying his grandchildren? If he had just left the humans to their own shit, he'd be here and not six feet under. And the press wouldn't let us alone either. Every year we'd have to hide away. And now she repays us with this? This is how she treats us after we did all this for her? Damn it all—"

"That's enough." There was command in Hunter's voice, enough that William dropped to his knees and bowed his head. "Get out of this house, and you are not to ever return. I will be contacting your Alpha as well, as I'm sure you have not notified him of you being here. Have you?"

"No, sir." William peeked at her. "She's still going to do this, isn't she? She's going to humiliate me and my family even though we didn't want this shit in the first place."

Slone stood up and moved to stand next to William. Her heart was broken...not because of what she'd done to him, but because he'd hated her more than she'd realized. But she could fix that right now.

"As of now you are no longer to have any contact with me or my companies. In the morning I will have the papers sent to you that absolves you of anything that you owe me. Included in it will be the deed to your house and a substantial bonus for all the years you were saddled with me. As of this moment you are no longer employed by any of my companies, and any hardships that you feel you have had to endure will have to be in the form of the check rather than me telling you again, as I have over the years, how much I appreciated you." He looked up at her, and she felt the tears threaten. "Had you ever once told me what you thought, I would have done things differently. I would have found somewhere else to live, I would have gone to another home and been raised by them. Cash is right. You hurt me in more ways than you say I hurt you. The difference is, you've been well compensated, while I have not."

"So, because of all this, you're firing me. What the hell am I supposed to do to make the kind of money you were paying me? You're not being fair about this, Slone. I did raise you." He started to stand but looked at Hunter, then stayed where he was. "What am I supposed to do now?"

"I don't care. And I'm being more than fair, William. I've compensated you for years for what you were doing for me. I've purchased you a home, the boat you use once a month to bring me things. I've paid for all the boys to go to college, paid for your cars, vacations, as well as anything and everything else you ever asked me for. For a man who was suffering overly much for taking me in for a dozen years, you've done very well for yourself. At my expense."

"If they come to us, even a hint of our name is brought up during this debacle that you're creating, I will own you." Slone laughed at William, and he stood up. "You think this is funny? Listen to me, bitch, I will sue you for everything you have."

His hand came out to no doubt slap her, but it was caught in mid-air. She watched as Hunter pulled William's arm up behind him and forced him back to the floor.

William opened his mouth, but Hunter pulled his arm up higher and William cried out.

"This is my mate, you fucking idiot. My Alpha mate. And you were going to hit her. Do you know what I could do to you right now?" William cried out when Hunter showed him what he could do. "You should be dead right now, but I'm not going to do that to you. What I am going to do is make a call. A few of them. And if you think you were going to have trouble finding something that paid well before, I got news for you...you're not going to have shit when I'm finished."

"She owes me." William spit at her and that was all it took to have Hunter move. It was over so quickly that she wasn't sure what she saw until William was out the door and laying in the yard. Slone put her fingers in her mouth and issued a shrill whistle. Her buddy and his pack seemed to move out of the shadows and were standing before her before she put her hand down.

"This is William Giles. I want you to get his scent, and if you smell him anywhere near this property, or for that matter anywhere around this town again, you have my permission to do with him as you please. He is not welcome here." The wolf that she'd been friends with growled low in his throat as he looked at William. When he started to stand, one of the pack leapt at him and knocked him down. Slone laughed. "I think they want you to crawl on your belly like the snake you are."

Turning her back on the scene in the yard, she looked at the men who had come to her rescue. They were still pissed, she could see that, and she was never more proud of any sight in her life. She kissed each of them on the cheek, saving Cash for last.

"You're my hero. Was it you that called for Hunter or one of the others?" He blushed brightly. "Thank you. I'm not sure…I think you are the greatest man I know."

He blushed brighter, and she kissed him again. She looked at Luke. He was going to hate her but not like William did. She shut her heart and mind to him for now.

"I want you to take over the mayoral position, please?" He started to tell her no, she just knew it, but she cut him off. "This town needs a man who knows the law, has no reason to steal from the funds, and who will be fair to both humans and wolf."

"I appreciate the offer, but I'm not sure that I'm cut out for that sort of thing. I do better one on one." She nodded and waited. "Really, I don't want the job. It's very nice of you to think of me, but I really don't want it."

"You'll have to take over as soon as we get this guy out, you know. I'd like to buy you a new desk, too. The one that's in that office now is not suited for you. I'll look later tonight online."

He looked at Hunter. "She's going to make me do it, isn't she?" Hunter laughed and patted his brother on the back, leading him from the room. She looked at Jarrett.

"Oh no, you don't. I don't know what's going on in that pretty little head of yours, but you just keep away from me." He ran out of the house before she could tell him she needed him to open a computer shop for her. Slone turned to look at Cash.

"You do know that they'd do just about anything for you, right?" She sat down and shook her head at him. "Well, darlin', you're very wrong about that. I think…no, I know that each and every one of them would take a bullet for you. They have fallen as much in love with you as I have."

"You love me, too?" She knew that she sounded whiney, but it had been a hard day so far. "I've never really had anyone to tell me that since…well, since my dad. You kind of remind me of him sometimes. Like when you call me darlin'. He never called me that, but he called me his punkie-doodle. I'm not sure why he did that, but he did." Cash nodded and smiled. "I love you, too, Cash. I mean I really do. You've given me so much and have asked for nothing in return. I don't think anyone has ever done that for me."

"You stick with me darlin' and you and I will make things work. And we'll bring them boys of mine around, too." He leaned on the table, taking another scone. "You thinking Luke will make a good mayor, huh? Me too. Me too. He's got a good head on his shoulders and he likes to think outside of them boxes. I just love it. And what do you have planned for Lee? That boy can cook, just so you know. Jarrett would do well in any setting, so long as there's a pretty girl or two and a place for him to be able to tinker."

She told him that she had a computer company and that they were wanting to sell out and move on to something else. "Jarrett fixed my computer for me in just under an hour. He said that it was his dream someday to be his own boss. And the computer store here in town leaves a lot to be desired." She flushed. "I know a little about them, just enough to get me into trouble, but I've a great respect for them."

"You might be right about that. We'll have to work on him for a little while, I think. But I don't think you're going to be able to pull Ellis away from the company. He's had his heart set on that since he was a teenager. Graham? I'm not sure about what he likes most. He dabbles in a great many things. But I'd say his passion...well, that would be wildlife, mostly aquatic."

She was making mental notes as they talked about each sibling. Slone had a guess that Cash would be happy just working each of their lives around to suit himself, but she didn't say anything. She decided that she wanted him with her, in the garden or anywhere else he wanted to be. By the time she'd convinced Lee to make them dinner, she had an idea for each of the men in her life.

~~~

"This makes no sense whatsoever." Ben looked up at Wagner, who was sitting there in the chair like he had nothing better to do than to stare at him. "Are you listening to me? I said this makes no sense. Does it to you?"

"Yes, it does. The first list is of the people that she wishes you to invite to the press conference. And with that is a list of alternatives in the event that this first list doesn't want to attend or is unable. I have already contacted them per Mr. Emerson, and every one of them has agreed to attend. The second list is the news stations that have been invited, and the green check near the name is those that have said they would come." Ben noticed that every one of the names were checked. "The second list is the names of the newspapers that have been invited to attend. I have checked the ones that are coming in the same manner."

Again all the names were checked. There were well over two hundred news sources on this list, and he had yet to look at the one where special guests had been asked. He looked up at Wagner and frowned. This seemed like a lot of work accomplished, and he'd only just gotten the list this morning.

"Did you have this list before I did?" Wagner smiled and nodded. "And just how the hell did you have it before me? Did you come in and get it off my computer before I got here?"

Ben had been coming into work on time since Miss Morris had blindsided him. He'd even been staying until five most nights as well. It put a crimp in his social life, of course, but until she left town, he was going to work hard at impressing the bitch.

"Mr. Emerson gave me an advanced copy and asked me to work on it. He said that the sooner we have a count, the better it will be on the booths that are being organized. Did you know that already we have fourteen different groups bringing in food and drinks? I suggested that we make it a sort of street fair, and he agreed. I think it will be nice for the communities. Don't you?" Ben wanted to get up, go around his desk, and bitch slap the man. Where the hell did he get off suggesting anything to this man? He should have told him first so that he could have presented it to him. Now he just looked stupid.

"I will be informed from now on when you have private conversations with Emerson. I don't care if he calls you in the middle of the night, you call me and let me know what the hell is going on." Wagner nodded, but he wasn't sure he was going to do it. "I mean it, Wagner. If I even have a hint that you're going to this man, I will fire you."

"Oh, that reminds me." He reached into a file that was still on his lap and pulled out a white envelope. He handed it to Ben with a big grin. "This is my resignation notice. As you can see, it has been witnessed and dated. If you think to fire me before the end of my time, then I will sue you. If you decided to give me leave with pay to finish out my notice, then know that I have everything that is going on with this large money making event on my thumb drive, and when I leave, it goes with me. Every last appointment, every one of the contact people that I've talked to, and the information that Miss Morris had seen fit to give me to help me expedite this event."

Ben opened the envelope, steaming pissed. The nerve of this little pisser. This was blackmail plain and simple. And according to this, his notice ended the day of the event. Which, glancing at his calendar, was in three days.

"You're not going to get away with this. I'm pretty sure there is some clause in my contract with you that states that you must give me a full two weeks." Wagner shook his head. "No you don't, or no you're not going to fulfill it?"

"I have no contract with you at all. I have one for the county that states that I will not share information I might obtain while working for them, not you. But it only covers things that could and would harm the county. If you were to…let's say if you were to take some of the county money and do something like go to dinner with your family and write it off as a business dinner, or say you use the county car for vacationing, then I would be obligated to report that. As I have done."

"You did what?" Wagner stood up when he did. Ben's mind was going over everything this prick knew about him, and he was coming up on the short end of the stick. Christ, he was going to be out of a job if he even told them half the shit he did. Daily. "When did you start this little campaign of yours to have me impeached? You couldn't have been doing it all along."

"Since Miss Morris asked me to do so." Wagner gathered up his file and left the one with the event information on his desk. Ben thought about shredding it all but figured someone as efficient as he was, Wagner would have back-ups of back-ups. He was so fucked right now.

Ben looked around the office and tried to think where the hell he'd gone wrong. "The moment you took office. Maybe even before that."

He had, too. Ben had cheated at college to get better grades. Not just good grades but ones that gave him the key to anything he wanted. College had been nothing but a blur of drinking, fucking, and smoking. And not necessarily in that order. And when he'd graduated, because he'd had a little knowledge of the system they used, he'd graduated with honors and not the straight fails he'd actually gotten in school.

He was still trying to think how he could fix this when his phone rang. Ben answered it on the second ring. Closing his eyes when he realized who it was, he nearly hung up on the man.

"Mr. Conklin? It's Luke Emerson. I was wondering how you are coming along with your list. Allen has done a wonderful job in keeping me abreast of what he's been able to accomplish is such a short amount of time." Ben asked him who Allen was. "Your assistant. Allen Wagner. You do know who works for you, don't you?"

"Of course I do. I just never call him by his first name. He's just Wagner to me." Ben realized how lame that sounded and changed the subject. "I wasn't aware there was a list for me to do. I just assumed with your all secret meetings with *my* assistant that he was doing it all for you." He'd been childish in emphasizing his assistant, but he was feeling particularly snarky right now.

"I assure you, Mr. Conklin, that I have had very public meetings with—" Ben cut him off. He'd had enough of this bastard, too.

"It's Mayor Conklin, not mister. You might want to remember that when we're before the cameras. I'm mayor of this county and what I say goes. If I wanted to shut down this little thing your mistress has coming up, don't think I wouldn't hesitate in one second to do so. I'm in charge and she might want to remember that." Ben was startled to hear laughter. Before he could ask him what the hell was so funny, Emerson spoke again.

"All right, *Mayor* Conklin. Does that make you feel better? I should hope so. And as for you threatening to shut things down, I would think very hard and very long on that. In the event you haven't noticed, the governor, a man that is in a better position than you are even on your best days, is going to be here. As are other men of state and local government. I would suggest — and that is all this is, a suggestion. I would suggest you get your head out of your ass, straighten the fuck up, and keep your fucking mouth shut before I have to come down there and shut it up for you. You mother fucking idiot. What the hell is...you know what? I don't care what you were thinking. Stop doing it. It's dangerous to your health."

The line was dead before Ben could think of a snappy reply. He sat at his desk with his head in his hands until he heard his phone ring. He didn't answer it but got up and moved around his office. Christ, he was going to be out of a job soon and he had no idea what the hell he was supposed to do now.

Ben had money, of course, but he'd never been one to save for a rainy day and it was fucking pouring right now. There wasn't even a place for him to live when he was fired. And there was no doubt in his mind right now that he was on his way out. In addition to having no house, he didn't even have a car to sleep in when he was homeless.

143

Mother fuck, this was really going to fuck up the rest of his life. Looking at the walls, he tried to tell himself that his lack of awards and accolades from the citizens was because he was not a very sociable person. But the truth of the matter was, he was a fucking prick. Always had been and would more than likely always be one.

He had to do something. Ben had no idea what at this point, but he had to get in good with the Morris bitch and see that she saw him as a good old country boy and not some asshole that was going to fuck up her day in the lime light. Ben went back to his desk. He had a list and he'd better get started on it. But the first thing on the list stumped him.

"How the hell do I make sure there is extra security on hand?" He looked at the phone number he had for the chief of police. He and Barker were drinking buddies. Perhaps he could lend him a hand. But the call to his office proved to be less than helpful. And a bit embarrassing. Barker had died a year ago.

Yeah, Ben thought, he was a fucked man. And not even a smoke to enjoy after she was finished with him.

Chapter 10

Hunter watched Slone. She'd been out in the yard since before the sun came up and she was still working at two in the afternoon. Lee had taken her out a sandwich, he'd told him, but he could see that it was still on the little table that held two bottles of water and an apple. He was beginning to really worry about her. If she was this stressed now, he could only imagine what she would be like tomorrow at the press conference.

"Honey?" She didn't look at him but kept digging at something in the dirt. Hunter walked up behind her and put his hands over hers on the hoe and held her. "You're going to hurt yourself. You have to eat something."

Slone leaned back against him and that's when he noticed the blood on her hands. Peeling them away, he could see that she'd had blisters and that those had popped and were now raw open wounds. He doubted, from the look on her face, that she'd even noticed them. Taking her hands to his mouth, Hunter licked the wounds, then picked her up. She didn't even fight him when he sat down at the table with her on his lap.

"Tell me what's going on." She just let him hold her and he looked out over the yard to the beach. "Okay, I'll talk to you until you come back to me. Did you know that my mom used to love the water? I think that's where Graham got it from. He was just a kid when she passed away. But he would go with her when the rest of us couldn't. They'd come back with bags of crabs and shells. I think he might have a few of them still."

Hunter thought of the last time she'd been to the beach. His mom had wanted to spend her last days out in the sun, and his dad had carried her down to the water's edge every day. Then one sunny day while they'd been building sandcastles with her watching over them, she'd fallen asleep and simply died. Hunter told Slone.

"She was something else. You kind of remind me of her at times. She was stubborn, too. But she was a good woman. And, boy oh boy, could she make me feel about one inch tall when I'd done something wrong."

"I bet you rarely did anything wrong that she'd caught you at." Hunter looked down at Slone when she spoke. "I bet you had her wrapped around your fingers."

"Nah, that was Jarrett. He could charm her into about anything. He could even get her to take us to the movies and see something no kids our age should have seen. Not sex, but violence. Then she'd tell us that most of that stuff was fake and that we should never think we can do any of those things to people and expect them to get up and make another movie like they did." Hunter kissed Slone on the mouth. "You should have something to eat. And try really hard not to scare the shit out of me like this."

"I didn't ask Willie to save me." He nodded, knowing that she was bothered by what William had said to her yesterday. Hunter wanted to go and find him and beat the ever living shit out of him. "I would gladly have given up my life had I known that he was going to die helping me. I didn't even know he was a person or what he was. I just thought he was a big wolf that was nice."

"My dad said that Willie was a nice man. Said he didn't have a great deal of respect for his only son, but he loved him. Dad said that if Willie was alive right now, he'd kill William for the things he'd said to you." Slone sat up, and he handed her part of the sandwich. "I thought you should know that Jess Giles, William's wife, has called here five times for you. She's pretty pissed at you. Basically saying that you gave them a lifestyle and she thought you should continue keeping them in that fashion. Luke said she claimed that you didn't give them near enough for all the hurt they were going to have to endure and the things they were going to have to give up. How much did you give them?"

"Two million." She reached for the bottle of warm water and drank it down before she continued. "Do you suppose there will be a time when they can look back on what I've actually done for them and say, 'oh yeah, we were better off with her in our lives'? I doubt it. I just realized that I'm grieving over something that was no fault of mine."

"No, you're grieving over a lost friendship. Or at least what you thought was a friendship." Hunter handed her the other half of the sandwich and smiled when she ate it like she was starved. She polished off the apple in no time. "We can go in the house and raid the fridge if you want. Since you have given Lee permission to stock the thing, there is all manner of food in it."

"I'm starved." Hunter nodded, and she smiled at him. A smile that made his cock leap in his jeans. "I mean, I'm really starved, Hunter. I don't suppose we could find us a nice quiet place and make it very noisy?"

"Fuck." He stood up with her still in his arms and tried to think where to go. He saw the shed and knew that it led to the beach and headed toward it. When his dad yelled for him, Hunter told him he'd be back later. Then the sound of laughter had him realizing that his dad knew what was going on. By the time they were going down a long stone staircase, Slone had turned in his arms and wrapped herself around him.

"There's a pool at the bottom of the stairs to your left." He turned to his left, and she laughed. "Okay, my left. But be careful. There is water everywhere."

Hunter turned and made his way back to the left when she started unbuttoning his shirt. When her mouth made its way down to his nipple and she bit him, he had to stop moving or fall over. Christ, if he made it another foot, they'd be lucky. But he took the next turn and stopped anyway.

"This is...Christ, this is amazing." In the center of the large room-like cave was a large pool. Hunter had no idea how deep it was, as the water was as clear as the sky. He sat her down when she asked him to, and she led him around the cavernous room. When she pointed upward, he looked.

There was a large hole that let the sun come down from above, and it was what made the stones and water seem so bright. He could see years of stalagmite growth from the floor. The art of it, the beauty of all of them, made the room look like a wonderland of nature. Even the stalactites that dipped like long ice icicles of mineral had formed into structures that made the cave unique to all others. He looked at Slone as she watched him.

"You come here a lot, don't you?" She nodded but still didn't say anything. "It's beautiful, and I thank you for sharing it with me."

"The water is warm year round for some reason. I think there might be a pocket of something under the water that does it. Nothing comes in here, like animals or anything. I think the wolves that run over my property keep them out. I've never even seen a snake in here." She moved to the water's edge, and Hunter wished he could paint. He would paint her just as she was now, a nymph just on the edge of diving into the pond.

"Come here, Slone. I want to strip you down and taste every part of you before I make love to you." She shook her head and stood up. His heart skipped several beats as she moved toward him. "Do you know what you do to me?"

"I do. It's the same that you do to me. But I want to be the one who tastes. I want to explore your body from top to bottom and everything in between." She had taken off his shirt as they'd moved down the cave. She looked him in the eyes when she put her fingers into his neckline of his tee-shirt and ripped it from him. As he started to reach for her, she told him no. "Don't distract me yet. I want to touch you."

As she touched him, her fingers gently moving over his body in the barest of touches, he held himself still. He'd never been a very patient man, but he would be for her. For as long as he could. When she stepped behind him and ran her hands up his ribs and to his chest, he stretched out his arms and waited for her to do whatever it was she wanted.

"You have the most amazing skin. It looks so hard, but it's so smooth and pliable. I love the fact that when you take me, I can dig my fingers into your flesh and hold on." He growled low, and she laughed a little. "I would never hurt you. I think I might be falling in love with you."

"I do love you." She came around him then and put her hands on his belt. But she slid her hand down the front of his trousers and wrapped her hand around him, and his breath caught. "Christ, you're going to kill me. I want you to hurry up, but I love what you're doing to me as well."

Sliding her hand free, she worked open his belt, then his pants. He hadn't touched her yet, but every part of him wanted to. Instead, he curled his hands into tight fists and tried to breathe slowly. He thought this was far and away the hardest thing he'd ever done.

When his pants were down around his thighs, he noticed that she didn't touch him. Not his skin or his cock, which was aching to be released. Her cheek brushed over his thigh, her hair danced along his skin, and he had to count backwards from a thousand to keep from leaping on her. As he held her head when she helped him remove his pants, he curled his fingers tightly, wondering what she was going to do next. She looked up at him from her kneeling position.

"I want to suck on your cock." He nodded, probably a little too eagerly. "I've never done this before so if I hurt you, will you tell me?"

"You can't hurt me. But I might hurt you once you take me into your mouth. I want to fuck you so badly that I'm nearly ready to come just from thinking about it." She nodded and leaned into his boxer-covered cock. Instead of touching him, as he wanted more than his next breath, she slid her hands up his boxers and ripped them off, just as she'd done his tee-shirt. "Slone, honey, I'm not going to last much longer."

"I've not touched you yet." He nodded and rocked his hips into her, trying to get her to take his cock, and she smiled. "Would you like for me to taste you now?"

"Yes." He hissed at her and nearly fell back when she took him into her mouth. He fucked her mouth as gently as he could. When she curled her hands around his ass and held him still, he tried to slow. But she was hot and wet and her tongue was doing things to him he'd never thought of before. As he stood there, having his cock swallowed over and over, he reached out to the wall next to him and held on. When he came—and it would be much sooner than he wanted, he knew as surely as he was standing there—he was going to fucking pass out from it. When she cupped his balls and rolled them into her palms, Hunter threw back his head and howled. His beast cried out as well as he filled her with his seed. Hunter held her to him as he felt his cock fill again. When he pulled back from her, she reached for him and he backed away.

"Bend over. He has to fuck you now." She stood up and nearly fell, but he grabbed her and nearly tossed her to the ground. He ordered her to shift just as his wolf took him. He entered her hard as soon as her wolf appeared, and he fucked her like the animal he was. The wolf wanted her to be his. Marking her, mating with her was all he could think about. When she tightened around him, her wolf coming hard, his wolf sank his canines into her shoulder and felt bones shatter under his bite. The more she cried out, her wolf screaming at him from beneath him, the harder his wolf took her until he felt his release take him. As soon as he came, his body nearly spent, he threw back his head and howled as well, telling whoever was close that he'd taken his mate.

~~~

Slone sat across from Hunter as they lay in the pool. She had never brought anyone down to this part of the cave before and was glad now that she'd not even shared it with William. This would be their special place from now on. When he laughed suddenly, she looked at him.

"You tore off my clothes and I'm officially naked when it comes to going back to the house." She had clothing down here, of course, but he didn't. "I suppose we could stay down here until dark. Then you could sneak me into the house. What do you think?" He ran his fingers over the scar that his wolf had given her. She'd been surprised by how quickly it healed, but he told her that he felt bad for it. She told him it was kind of sexy and laughed when he swatted her ass.

"I have a towel we can wrap around you. And if anyone asks we'll just tell them I raped you." He stared at her for all of five seconds before he laughed again. She had been making a joke and was glad that she'd done it. "You should laugh more often. Me, too, I suppose. But I've been so alone for most of my life that I guess I thought I had little to laugh about."

"I love you." She nodded. As much as she thought she loved him, she was still afraid to share that part of herself. "I can wait, you know. Just because I say it to you doesn't mean you have to say it back. Like I said, I can wait."

Nodding, she decided to change the subject. "I've about talked Luke into the mayoral job. I think he's already hired himself an assistant. He's the guy that is working for Conklin. Luke asked me to have a check run on him. So far he's come back pretty clean. Now Conklin, he's another story all together."

"Such as." She watched him swim over to her and waited for him to sit beside her before she answered him.

But he picked her up and put her on his lap instead. She was really getting used to all this touching thing. He reminded her that he'd asked a question.

"Oh. My investigator has heard from a couple of the professors at the college he went to. They would swear that he never studied at all the entire time he was there, and yet his grades reflected something altogether different. And when he asked them what his grades had been like, it seems that all his records as well as a few other people had been erased. I hope you don't mind, but I asked Jarrett to fly out there and see if he could help them."

"I see. And this firm that you're using, is it the same one that is selling out to you? And the same company that you want to expand into something closer to home?" She flushed, and he laughed. "I can read you like a book. I bet Jarrett jumped at the chance."

"He did sort of. I don't think he realizes that I've done this to bait the hook for him, but he went. I think he's sort of afraid of me." She turned in his arms and looked at him. "Why do you suppose he's afraid of me? I'm very harmless."

His laughter bounced off the walls and back to them. The sound was wonderful, and she found if she could simply stay here with him she'd do it. But life had a way of needing you sometimes.

"You, my love, are far from harmless. You wouldn't hurt him or any of them, but you are devious in a very roundabout way. Like Luke. He thinks that taking this position is for a short term, only until you find someone to take the job." She started to tell him it was, it's just that Luke didn't realize he was the man for the job. "Oh you don't have to explain to me that he'd be good at the job, but he will figure it out eventually."

"I'm hoping by then he'll love it so much that he'll simply bow down to my wishes." Hunter laughed again. "And I'm not devious, thank you very much. I'm just better at the business thing than most people are."

"Business thing, huh? You have managed to turn a great deal of wealth into an empire. I think this thing, as you call it, is a natural for you. I'm very proud of you. But we still need to see that owner's box. I have a schedule all printed out for us when we get some time." She knew that he had it, she'd seen it yesterday on the desk. Instead of telling him they were going to a game on Sunday, she stood up. He growled at her, but she knew it was nothing more than his wolf.

"I need to get to the house. I have several meetings soon and I can't be late for them." She had two with her attorney and one with her banker. She also had some work she needed to do about replacing William.

"I would like to sit in on them with you, if you don't mind." She nodded, knowing that he'd need to be there for at least one of them. And he was not going to be thrilled when he found out. "And I would like for you to sit with me on a meeting with a couple of the townspeople." She felt her body tense up.

"I don't know if I'm ready to do that." He nodded as he moved by her and opened the large chest she'd put down here. "I mean, I'm okay with you guys right now, but I'm still worried about what they'll think about me. I know that sounds really stupid, but I'm still nervous around lots of people."

"It's only three and if you don't want to come, that's fine as well. Mable is going to be there. As is Pete. You know Pete, or know of him." She nodded, not understanding why he wasn't pissed that she wasn't helping him with being an Alpha. "Oh, and that kid you helped with the wheelchair. They wanted to talk to us about the booths you're setting up."

"Just those three?" Hunter nodded as he wrapped the towel around him and handed her a tee-shirt and lounge pants. "You won't lead me into something I'll hate, will you?"

"Never." She stared at him but she was afraid, and she was pretty sure he knew it. Nodding once, he kissed her on the nose and helped her pick up their torn clothing. As they came out of the shed on her land, she noticed three things almost at once.

The wolves had a man cornered. A larger wolf, more than likely one of Hunter's brothers, had shifted, and Graham was lying on the ground unconscious. She ran to them as Hunter dropped the towel and shifted. She looked down at William when the wolf at his throat let him go.

"What are you doing here? I thought we'd settled this." He glanced to his right, and she saw the gun. "You came here to shoot me?"

"You fucking bitch, you can't do this to me." Slone felt the air tighten and put her foot on his neck. William shifting now would get him killed.

"You do and I will let every one of these wolves have you for dinner." He nodded, but she didn't let him go just yet. "What is it you think I'm doing to you? You're the one that severed this relationship. Not me. I would have been just as happy to not know what you felt about me."

"You killed my father." She pressed harder on his throat when he started to scream again. When she let up, he glared, but she knew he was as close to the edge as he'd ever been. "Jess is leaving me. And that's your fault, too. She found out about the other women and the gambling and she's leaving me. You cutting me off when you did was fucked up. How am I going to pay that debt off? Give me that job back and I'll forget the whole thing."

"Are you fucking serious? You gambled away all the...Christ, William. You had affairs too? And for the record, I had shit to do with your wife leaving you. Perhaps you should have thought of that before you came here spouting off that shit you did a few days ago."

She saw Cash helping Graham up and noticed that he seemed to be okay but for the bump on his head. Slone looked back at William. He was a pathetic man, and she wondered why she'd never seen it before.

Because you simply didn't think he'd feel this way. Slone glanced at Hunter as he stood beside her, his big wolf leaning into her leg. *You're an Alpha, love, his Alpha as long as he is here in our territory. You need to deal with him now or he will continue to come here and piss us all off. And he hurt one of my brothers. Had he been anyone but the man who raised you, I would have been well within my rights to kill him.*

Deal with him? How was she supposed to deal with him? Her first thought was to give him more money, but that would only make him want more. His wife was leaving him because he'd been gaming and seeing other women. She glanced at Graham as he stood on her other side. And he'd hurt one of her brothers.

"You're really fucked up, did you know that?" William looked at her and as soon as he looked like he was going to yell at her about some injustice she'd done to him, she pushed her foot harder into his neck. "I'm not finished talking yet, and you'll listen to me for a change. Now. You have two choices as far as I can see. One, I let Graham kill you. I can see by the look on your face that you don't believe me, but I'm not kidding. Shift, Graham."

He did so without hesitation. As he stood near her, growling deep in his throat and showing his sharp canines, William tried to get away. Slone pressed harder until he stopped struggling. Then he looked at her, and she could see the hatred in his eyes.

"The second choice you have is this. You get the fuck off my land and never return. If you do, and I mean to even come up on the beach below this house, I will send a pack of wolves after you. And there will not even be a bone fragment to bury when they're done. And so you know, I will make it my life's work to keep an eye out for you. To be honest, I hope you try it. I think the pack will enjoy a nice little snack." The big wolf, the one she called Buddy, snapped at William and bit deep into his leg. William screamed like a little girl, and the wolf howled back at him. The scent of blood was fueling the other wolves, too. Slone snapped her fingers and they all settled to the ground except for Buddy.

"And number three. I know that I didn't mention three, but it just came to me." She leaned down and smiled at him. "You threaten, hurt, or even look like you might want to hurt a member of my family again, and I will kill you. I will not be hesitant about it either, as I tear your throat out and spit it at you as you bleed to death. Do you believe me?"

"Yes." She nodded and stood up, lifting her foot up and moving back. But before she could get out of his reach, he leapt at her, shifting at the same time. All she felt was the wind being knocked out of her, pain in her arm, the sounds of a gun firing, and bones being snapped between growls and screams.

Chapter 11

"Yes, I understand what you're saying, but I assure you that it's not necessary. My mate is fine, if only a little pissed that someone else killed him before she could." Hunter turned to look at Slone as she sat on the couch. She was mad but mostly at him. She was upset that he could have been hurt when the gun went off. He'd called the other Alpha as soon as he figured out that his family was fine.

"You should just let me compensate you in some way, Alpha. I knew that William was having problems. Hell, the entire pack did. But to come to your home and try to kill you? I just never saw it coming." Hunter had, as had his dad. That was why they had been keeping an eye on Slone. He'd even tried talking to the other wolves. But they had saved his ass today so he figured they understood him well enough.

"I'm very serious when I tell you that my wife is hurting badly enough about this. If you insist on doing something, I would suggest that you do something for your own pack in memory of William and his family. His wife didn't need to be killed by him."

When Hunter had called the Alpha, his only thought was to make the man pay. But the moment that he'd told him who he was, the man had started sobbing. Apparently, Jess Giles had been his only daughter and William had murdered her in a fit of rage. She, apparently, was going to go back home to live with her father when William had come home. It was why he'd shown up here, Hunter supposed. To kill Slone, as he had blamed her for it all.

"I'll do that. My daughter would...the boys aren't taking it well. They moved away some time ago when they realized what their daddy was doing against their mom. Never did cotton to William much. Not a thing like his daddy was. There was a man worth having in your pack. Never went a day without helping out somebody. And when he was in that accident that bummed up his heart, did he slow down? Nope. He kept going like it was his business."

Hunter wondered if Slone knew that Willie had had a bad heart before he'd met her that day, and decided to tell her when he got off the phone. Right now, she was staring at the computer she had on her lap, but he doubted she was seeing it. Hunter hung up a few minutes later, assuring the man once again that money was not necessary. Hunter sat next to Slone.

"I think we should get some new furniture." She turned the computer toward him. "Something like this, I think. I never really cared much for decorating and simply used what I had, but if we're going to have people over for meetings, things should look nice. Don't you think?"

"I do." He took the laptop from her and looked at the furniture she'd been looking at. It was something he'd like, too. Dark and earthy tones along with deep reds and darker shades of golds and browns. The couch looked like leather, the two armchairs like a person could sink down in them and sleep for hours. Hunter wanted to ask her what this meant but didn't want to spoil the mood.

"And we need a new bed. I know that the one we're using now is kind of smallish for you, but there's this company that can make about any size you want. Do you have a preference about the furniture we have?" She opened another tab, and he put his hand over hers. She looked at him.

"Would you be willing to go and look at furniture? We could go in after they close and look around at our hearts content." She nodded, then shook her head. "Ordering from a computer, honey, just doesn't sound like we'll get what we want."

"I'm terrified. I know you understand that, but you can't...I want to work on getting out. I started to say again, but I don't think I've really been out. I buy things online because I can. I've never put much thought into what it might feel like or really look like. I needed it and there it was. The only time I've ever actually shopped for something that I wanted was that tractor. Do you know how much fun it was for me?" He nodded and pulled her into his arms. "And I think that...I think that knowing that it wasn't all my fault helps. William hurt me as much...more I think...than I did myself. I'm not blaming him entirely, but like Cash said, if he had gotten me help then maybe I'd be different."

"Maybe, but I think you're perfect the way you are." She said nothing and he held her for a little while longer. It wasn't until his dad came into the room and stood in front of him that he realized she'd fallen asleep.

"I have to tell you something. You might already know it, but I don't think so." His dad spoke in low tones, but he had no problem hearing him. "I know she said that she can't have children, but I think...she's breeding now. I thought so the other week, that she was in heat, but then today when the big wolf knocked her back but took care to see that she didn't hit the ground hard, I knew. I'd say she's going to have a baby sometime in late summer."

Hunter looked down at the bundle in his arms, then back at his dad, who just nodded. "I thought...the other day when I marked her. I thought she tasted different. I wasn't sure what it was but...a baby?"

"Yeah. It might be because you and she are mates, or the simple fact that you've completed the change in her, but her marks are gone, too, on her wrist. I know she had a couple of them, but I won't know if those are gone, too." Hunter tried to think if he'd seen them and had to be honest with himself, he just didn't see them any longer. Lifting her shirt up as easily as he could, he saw that the one on her belly was gone, too. Hunter felt his world brighten about a thousand times over.

A baby. They might be having a baby. He wondered how he could find out for sure without getting her hopes up, but his dad nodded and congratulated him. As far as Hunter was concerned, it was verified. Holding Slone just a little tighter, yet gentler, he thought of her huge with his child and couldn't stop smiling. Lee came in to call them to dinner and he finally woke her.

When she stood up, he did as well and then picked her up into his arms and swung her around the room. She was laughing with him when he sat her back on the floor. Pulling her into his body, he looked down at her.

"My dad is the most amazing man I know." She laughed and agreed with him. "Did you know that as a wolf, the female goes into heat and the male, her mate, is the only one who can impregnate her at that time?" She pulled away from him, and he could see her sadness.

"I wish I could give you a baby. The thought of a child of yours growing inside of me...you have no idea how much I would love that." He nodded and pulled her back. "I'm so sorry, Hunter. Maybe we can adopt a baby. I know it won't be the same, but we could raise it together as our own."

"You're pregnant." Slone looked up at him. "Dad told me. I mean, he said he thought you were in heat a couple of weeks ago, and today he said you were breeding...having a baby. We can tell very early in the pregnancy because of the scent you give off, but since I've never really been around a female during that time, I had no idea what it was. And you taste different."

"They told me that my womb was damaged beyond the ability to...I can't have a baby." She covered her flat belly with her hand and took a step back. "The doctors said it was impossible for me to conceive."

"Your scars are gone, too. The ones on your wrist and belly. I should look at the back of your leg, too, just to be sure, but when I'm looking at your rear end, I'm too busy pounding you from behind."

She looked down at her body and lifted her skirt. Even from where he was, he could see, like before, that the scar was gone. Slone sat down hard, and he dropped before her, watching her for any sign that she was upset about having his child.

"Do you think it's possible?" Hunter nodded. "I mean, I was surprised about how fast I healed in the pool this morning, and then...I never looked at the scars anymore, but they really are gone. What do we do now?"

"I don't know." He laughed and kissed her. "I suppose we'll have to shop for baby stuff when we go looking for living room furniture."

"A baby. Of our own." He kissed her again and laid her back on the couch. Lifting her shirt up, he kissed where his child was. His child was laying there all nested in his mother, and all Hunter wanted to do was go find his family and tell them. Hell, he wanted to shout it to the world. He was going to be a daddy.

During dinner, he was nearly ready to explode. His dad kept smiling at them, and his brothers kept looking at him like he'd lost his mind. It wasn't until apple pie was served that he finally couldn't take it any longer. He stood up and pulled Slone to her feet beside him.

"I have an announcement to make." They all turned to him and Hunter felt like he had the best of the world right there with him. "Slone and I are going to have a baby."

There was silence all around. Then Luke stood up and kissed her on the cheek. He looked at Hunter and smiled as he patted him on the back.

"No offense, big brother, but we knew this a few days ago. The way you two go at it all the time, it's small wonder you didn't have her knocked up the first day." Hunter looked at his dad when he laughed.

"How the hell did you know?" They all turned to Lee, who flushed. "You knew before I did? How?"

"Well, I did go to medical school for about a minute. And you might remember that we all live here, too. We can smell her as well as you can." He looked at his brothers, who were all nodding. "Sorry, bro, but you should really pay more attention to what's going on around you."

Sitting down now, sort of deflated, he looked at Slone when she smiled at them all. He wanted to pull her into his lap again and pout, but he didn't. He was too mature for that.

His mate, and soon-to-be wife, squeezed his hand. They'd talked for a long time today on things that she was going to tell his brothers and about what she'd done for him. As much as he wanted to be able to care for her, he wasn't so pigheaded that he didn't know that he could never do what she had already done for herself. He would let her do this part of their happy news. Because he knew from the meetings he'd sat in on this morning with her that she was indeed very business minded and knew just how to get things done.

"We have another announcement to make. I'm just hoping that...you're going to be pissed I know, but it's a done deal and you'll have to learn to live with it." She turned to his dad. "I have fallen in love with you. I'd very much like to call you 'Dad' if you don't mind. That's not what I have done for you, but — "

"Hell, yeah, you can call me 'Dad.' Shit fire and milk the cow. I have a daughter." His dad laughed. "You've given me more than I could ever thank you for, child. I feel it's an honor to have you call me that."

After a quick hug, she turned to Luke. "You really are going to hate me. We have secured you the position as mayor here. Not that it took much in the way of persuading people. They have decided that if you run or not, you will continue to be the mayor with write-in votes. In addition to that, we've set you up a campaign fund for later use, as well as paid off all your student loans and hired you as a consultant on my team."

"You didn't have to do that, Slone. Seriously. I was making headway in them." She nodded and kissed him on the cheek. "Hunter will kill me for this, but — "

Luke tipped her back and kissed her full on the mouth. When he pulled her back up, Hunter stood up and felt his wolf race along his skin. With a wink at him, Luke let her go and sat back down. After a few seconds, she turned to Jarrett.

"I don't want it." She nodded. "I don't know what it is you've done for me, but take it back. I love you just the way things are between us."

"Then you don't want to run the computer company that we've just acquired?" He stared at her for several seconds. "They couldn't make a go of it and no matter how many times I tried to get them to seek help, they simply wanted to do it their way. It's in the black now, but without proper management and a person who thinks outside the box on occasion, it will be like so many start-up companies I've helped. Dead before it got a good hold."

"Anderson Technologies?" She nodded. "They were too slow to get things transferred over to more advanced systems and the bus left them standing. What kind of capital will you lend, and I do mean lend, me to get it going?"

"We will give you any amount of loan you think you're going to need. And according to my business gurus, you will have to pay interest on it. It's only good business sense for all of us." Jarrett got up and pulled her to his body and kissed her on the cheek. He looked over at Hunter and winked as Luke had.

"I'll take my kiss later." With that he sat back down and finished his pie. They all turned to Ellis.

"You know what I want." She nodded. "We've talked and talked about it, but I don't think you can help me with it."

"But we have. As of now, you have nineteen employees that answer only to you. Dan and his men have decided that if they are going to make it in the construction world at all, they need someone who can pull them up. I'm not saying that in a few years you won't have some hefty competition, but for now, they want to work for you." He nodded but didn't move.

"What else?" She laughed and handed him a thick envelope. He looked at Hunter, and Hunter nodded. "You've done more than simply given me a start on a company that I want; what else have you done?"

"You are now sole owner of Emerson Construction. Inside that envelope is papers from each of your family members signing their part over to you. Your dad said it was your lifelong dream to make it work, and Hunter and I have given you a little boost. There are two contracts in there as well. One for the new library in town and one for the work on the new pack house. Each of them have a check attached so that you can get started as soon as you wish."

Ellis nodded and stood up. He simply stood there for a long while before he turned from the room and left. Hunter knew his brother well enough to know that he would need some time to absorb this. He did when she'd told him what he was to get.

He got it all. Not just her money, which she had insisted that he would have half of, but also any future money they'd make. There were the investments, too, that she'd put his name on. Hunter wasn't just half owner in her life, but a full partner. He liked that much better than simply being her husband and mate.

Lee grinned at her when she turned to him. "I have an all-expense paid ticket to the best cooking school in the world. I'll have spending money as well as a nice place to live." She nodded and Lee stared at her. "I'm kidding."

"I'm not. The cordon bleu college in France has a spot for you. But it's hinged on you being able to show them you're worth it. After that, you will have a place there to live, a spending account to help you study hard without worrying about bills, and a big kitchen to play in." Lee told her again he was kidding, and Hunter laughed.

"I don't think she is, little brother. I guess you will be starting soon, too. Like in four months." Lee stood up and sat back down. The look on his face was priceless, like he wanted to believe her, but he didn't want to get his hopes up. Hope was a very fragile thing.

"You really are doing this for me." Slone nodded, then shook her head. "I knew it was a joke. I knew that—"

"Not a joke. It's real. What I meant was, it's not for you. It's for me. I have some plans for you when you graduate. There are a number of failing or about-to-fail restaurants that I'd very much like for you to help with. Not cooking, but with your ability to do what others haven't been able to…charm the socks off the customers."

Lee stood up again, and just before he reached for Slone, he looked at Hunter. "You know that this means more to me than anything that I could ever have hoped for. The chance to be something, to make something of me."

"You are something to me, Lee. You always have been." Hunter hugged his brother with Slone between them. "And so you know, until you leave, you're in charge of the kitchen. It was the only thing I could get her to wait the four months for. Otherwise you would have been gone in the morning."

After Lee left them, Slone looked at Graham. He was already shaking his head, and Hunter knew that of all his brothers, he would be the hardest to get to accept what they'd been able to do for him.

"I know you mean well. And I really love you both for it, but whatever little tricks you have in your bag, I can't use it. Hunter probably already told you." Slone nodded, and Graham nodded. "I can help you around the house, and I want to work with Ellis, too. I could stand to lose a few pounds. But college is out of the question."

He'd told Slone, but his dad had already mentioned it to her. And in a few short hours, she'd gotten everything cleared up. It was as simple as calling in favors and having the money to back up the term.

"I want answers now."

"I called the university. Last week when I spoke with your dad." Graham nodded and stood up. "They have reinstated your grades and are honoring your scholarship."

"What?" He sat down again and looked at her. "That's not possible. I nearly had to serve jail time. I had to…they kicked me out for cheating and I didn't."

"You didn't, you're right. I had some people look into it. Did you know that when you left, nine other students were caught doing what you'd been accused of? Of cheating on their exams to keep their scholarships? And they all admitted who was in the ring with them. Not one of them mentioned you. But the university was too embarrassed to have it known that they'd made such a major mistake. Especially in light of what the college has to endure now that it's going to be public knowledge."

Graham stared at her, and Hunter had to laugh. The man was afraid to ask. Finally when he did, Slone handed him the file that she'd had faxed to her that morning.

"There will be no more donations given to them for a period of five years. Not from me nor a great many other contributors. It's not my idea but that of the college lawyers. And you will have your full scholarship as I have said, plus all your expenses paid by them. In addition, you will be awarded passing grades on all the classes you've already taken." Graham continued to stare at her and she nodded to him. "Neither your dad nor brothers ever believed you'd done this. Neither did I when I heard about what had been said. You're a wonderful man and you have the ability to do so much more. I hope you'll go back and finish."

"I have one year." Hunter nodded when he looked at him. "Not even a year left to finish, then I can...I can do what I want."

"We were afraid you'd turn us down. Say that you didn't want to go back there. But this is a good deal for you, Graham. Not only are you getting to go back to finish up, but you're getting your good name back. They are publically apologizing to you and are going to make good all the shit they did to you."

"My record, too?" Hunter nodded. "I couldn't even get a job. I had to...I've had to work for shit since this thing happened."

"I know." He'd worked for them in the summers, but it was never enough for him. Hunter knew that Graham had always had dreams of taking care of the oceans. But this, this was going to open a great many doors for him. And Slone and he were going to be able to help him.

"I want to do this on my own." Slone started to speak, but he cut her off. "I don't want your money. Not yet at any rate. I need...I feel like I have a second chance at this, a chance to prove myself, and I can't feel like I can with you backing me. Not that I don't appreciate it, but...." Graham looked at him.

"We understand and we already talked about it. But Slone and I...well, we still wanted to help you out. Since the university is in Florida, we have arranged for you to have a plane at your disposal. So you can come home to us. I can't stand the fact that Lee is going to be away for a while, Luke is going to be here but working all the time, and Ellis and his business will take him away for long periods of time as well. We want you all to come here when you can."

Graham hugged them both then left them. The only person left was Dad. He was wiping at his cheeks when Slone took his hand. He nodded twice before Slone spoke.

"Dad?" His dad stood up and pulled her into his arms for a hug. He kept saying that he was proud of her and that he couldn't love her more if she was his own. When he finally sat down, he kept holding her hand like it was a lifeline. "I love you."

"And I love you, too, darlin'. More than I could tell you. What you did for this family...what you have done for me...I'll never be able to repay you for it." Dad looked at Hunter. "You either. You made this old man proud."

"Will you stay with us?" He looked at Slone. "I mean forever. I want you to live with us. I know the others are moving out and moving into their own places, but I'd like...Hunter and I would love for you to stay here. I need help in the garden, and when the baby comes, I'll need help with him, too. Then there's the—"

"You serious?" She nodded. "Well, hell yeah, I'm staying. Best gift a man could have. A baby to bounce on my knee, a pretty woman in the kitchen cooking some scones, and someplace to play in the dirt. I'm a contented man."

He left them after that, and Hunter looked at Slone. "He should have stayed for the rest of it. I'm pretty sure he's going to throw a fit."

"He'll get over it. But he's staying now and that's all that matters." She looked around the room. "We're going to need a bigger table and more chairs."

Hunter agreed. They were growing by leaps and bounds, and he was so happy he could bust.

Chapter 12

Ben watched the chairs being set up and wandered over to one of the long tables that Miss Morris and a few others were going to be seated at. He'd been there since six-thirty that morning and it was just going on noon now. Ben decided that being mayor was not as bad as he'd always made it out to be. He was actually having fun.

"Mayor, there's a call from that newspaper in California again. He wants to know if he can have a front row seat if he pays you for it." Ben wasn't even tempted now to take it and have the guy fend for himself when he got there. It was amazing what the threat of losing your job could do for you.

"Tell him that there is no assigned seating; this is not high school. And also inform him that if he calls here again, I will make it my business to keep him out of this thing." Ben was sure he could do that, but it made the woman who was holding the phone smile. "Also, have you heard from Miss Morris? She was supposed to be here ten minutes ago."

"She's here. I think her and her entourage are in the hall. She's having some issues, I think." He started for the hallway when he saw the men first. "Yeah, they wouldn't let me in either. They said to wait."

The four men standing outside the ladies' bathroom looked like they might work for the Secret Service. They all wore dark suits like they had been tailored just for them, dark glasses, and they didn't even bother hiding the fact that they were all armed. Two had their guns at their hips, and Ben was reasonably sure they'd shoot first and fuck asking questions. He stood there waiting for some sign that he could see Miss Morris. One of the men turned to the door and opened it just as she came out. And damn, Ben swallowed three times before he remembered to shut his mouth.

To say the woman was beautiful would have been grossly understated. Of all the times he'd seen her, all the ways she'd looked, this was something he would never forget. The slim-fitting suit she had on complemented her pale skin like someone had made the color just for her. Her auburn hair was coiled up in one of those fancy knots that only a hair dresser could do, and her heels, all four inches of them, made her legs look longer than her entire body. Christ, she was gorgeous.

"Mr. Conklin, I've been hearing good things about you. They say that you've gotten off your ass and helped out more than we expected." He started to snap at her but held his tongue. He needed to keep his job, and she was the means to do it. "Is everything ready?"

"It is. There are some press already here. They started showing up last night, as a matter of fact. I thank you for the heads up on that. I don't know why, but I never expected them to be this early." She nodded and they moved as one down the hall, her guards around her and him standing within their circle. "All the arrangements you've asked for have been set up. And the 4-H booth has been doing a big business. Already this morning they sold out of coffee and donuts, and now some hot dogs are being sold as well. Mable has her pies on display and is doing a bang-up business there as well."

She nodded, and Ben wanted to ask her how he was doing with this as well. He felt stupid really, asking for approval from a woman, but this woman, he'd come to find out, was too powerful not to bow down before. When a man came toward them, two of the guards peeled away and pushed, although gently, Ben to a nice distance away from them. The couple embraced.

He was escorted to the gym again. It was show time in less than an hour and the place had really filled up since he'd been gone. There was not an open seat anywhere, and the line that had been put up to keep people from the big table was now being patrolled by three of the biggest dogs he'd ever seen. On second look, he realize they were wolves. Ben wondered if they would hurt anyone while this was going on, but noticed that while they did walk back and forth, they never looked at the people nearly on top of them. Ben made sure that things were ready and at ten minutes till the hour, several men came to the table and sat down. A few minutes later, Miss Morris did.

It was mayhem for about ten minutes. Cameras were going off and people were moving closer to the table. The wolves seemed to be keeping them from actually coming across the line, but it was close. Ben moved to stand next to Miss Morris, as he'd been told it was up to him to announce her.

Just before things settled, however, he was pulled from the detail and into the hall. The lawyer, Luke Emerson, was standing there with Wagner. This was not going to be good, he just knew it.

"To save you the embarrassment of a public firing and arrest, I've decided to do it here." Ben felt his world tilt as three cops came toward him. "Mr. Ben K. Conklin, you are under arrest for theft, money laundering, misappropriation of county and state funds, and use of a vehicle while not on official...are you all right?" Ben felt himself going down, not just his career but his body, too. As he was being helped to the floor, someone kept saying his name, and then he was slapped. He looked at Wagner.

"You did this to me." Wagner shook his head, but Ben knew better. "You fucked me in the ass and all because you have a burr up your ass about something. Did she pay you to spy on me? Is that it? She told you she'd give you all kinds of money and you did it?"

"No. I didn't do anything but keep track of you. It was my job, as you know. And as for Miss Morris paying me? No, she didn't. In fact, she asked me to resign from working for you so that I wouldn't have my job in question as well. She is a very nice woman, and I'm going to enjoy working for the new mayor." Ben asked if it was her, and Wagner laughed. "No, not her. But him."

He pointed to Emerson, and the man smiled. "You're the new mayor? Who appointed you the mayor? I have to be informed of these things. And you can't just take this from me. I've been doing a much better job. I even did what was on her fucking list for her."

"Yes, you did. However, it was the two terms previous that you fucked up." He was jerked to his feet when Emerson nodded to one of the police. "Mr. Conklin, I wish I could say it was great fun, but we both know it was not.

176

You will have a trial date in a few days and then we can proceed from there."

Ben was still yelling when he was shoved into the back of the cruiser. There were just enough cameramen hanging around that he was caught on tape. He was sure he was going to make a bigger headline than anything the tragic Miss Morris could say. As he was being taken away, he looked up and saw Wagner there. The fucking man even blew him a kiss just before he went back into the building. Ben wished now he'd just taken off three days ago when he'd realized how fucked he really was. Now it was simply too late.

~~~

Slone looked around the room trying to catch her breath. There were more people in this room than she realized it could hold. As her panic started to rise out of control, she tried her best to tell herself that this was a good thing. This was going to end it all, and she knew that she was going to throw up.

Just as she turned to Hunter to tell him she'd changed her mind, she saw the woman in the front row raise a sign. "Thank you" was all it said. Slone tried to think what she was thanking her for when the small handmade sign was flipped over. "Mable Carlyle of Mable's Fine Dining." Slone stared at her for several seconds, her befuddled mind working through who she was. When it occurred to her, she nodded once and the sign was laid back in the woman's lap. The man sitting next to her raised his. It, too, said "thank you" and the other side said "College tuition loan." Then a second sign was lifted which read, "Paid in full." She laughed, and Hunter looked at her. She nodded to the seats, and he smiled.

There were several more signs. Each of them started with "thank you" and ended with why she was being thanked. A wheelchair she'd helped get and the railing to his house. A desktop computer for the library and how it had saved countless hours in book research. There was one from a woman who patted her large belly. Slone had apparently helped her afford a car so she could make it to doctor appointments. Sign after sign was held up, and Slone acknowledged them all. She felt her first easy breath since she'd woken that morning.

Luke came from the back of the room and walked toward her. He nodded at her and winked, and she knew that he was now the acting mayor of Somerville. She was as ready as she'd ever be when he stood at the podium.

"Ladies and gentlemen, my name is Luke Emerson. I'm here today to introduce you all to Slone Morris Emerson. As of yesterday afternoon, this lovely lady became my sister-in-law and married my big brother, Hunter." He asked them to stand up, and they did. When everyone stopped cheering, he turned back to the crowd. "All of you have been given a list of rules. And as stated before you came here, she will answer all questions that she can. At no time will she hold back any information on that day from you as she knows it."

The first person to stand when the conference started was a young man that looked like he had all the answers and he was going to rip her apart. As soon as he asked his first question, "What did you really do to your father?" she knew it was going to be just fine.

"Nothing. I loved him with all my heart, worshiped him as a matter of fact, but I didn't do anything to him. He was dead before I was taken on that fateful trip."

The man nodded. "Are you saying that you had nothing to do with his death? That you didn't kill him with the help of your stepmother to gain the riches you now have?" He snorted. "I find that hard to believe, Slone. I mean, it was all very convenient that you inherited everything because they both just happened to be dead."

Hunter started to move, but she put her hand on his. "Convenient? How do you figure that? My mother, if you had researched any of my life prior to this, left me everything. He was never going to see any of her money. He couldn't manage it for me, he couldn't use it to care for me, and he had no way of even borrowing against it. He did, however, work hard for us, giving me a home and food on the table for a time. When he was gone for long periods of time, there were no nannies to care for me, no staff to cook for me. For a time, it was a paid sitter that came in every day, and then when he married…then—"

She didn't finish but stared him down. The next person was at the microphone in a minute. "Mrs. Emerson, congratulations by the way. I was wondering if you could tell us what your stepmother said to you that morning when she put you in the car? Did she hint to you that she was going to try and kill you?"

"No. And I wasn't just put into the car. I was caged." She looked at Lee, who was going to show pictures or whatever was needed. The police had been very helpful to her concerning this, and she also had the doctors there that had treated her for her injuries that day. "This is the back of the SUV that was parked in the lot just down from where I was found. As you can see, there's an animal cage and a small blanket over it. That was so that I couldn't see out and no one could see me inside. I would ride there, this way when she'd have to make trips to town. This is not to say that there wasn't another such cage at home."

Another picture came up, this one of the basement. It showed just a wire cage sitting up on cinder blocks with newspaper under it. She told how she'd be locked in the cage for a couple of days when Eva felt she'd done something to her. As they moved through the men and women asking questions, Slone hurt. Not just for her but that she'd had to do this. When another man stood up, she watched him as he thumbed through his notepad. Finally he looked at her.

"I was a reporter when you were found. I remember seeing this tiny little girl laying on this big rock and thinking to myself 'that could have been one of my little girls.' You were in such horrible shape. Bloodied and bruised, one tennis shoe hanging off your toes and the other gone. I wondered who could...why would anyone want to murder a child? And then I started hearing things about how you'd been in on a plot to kill your father, how you'd taken the money and ran. And how, years later, yet another story came out about you that you'd used the money to buy a mansion and had peons working for you for little to no money." He nodded as he put his notebook away. "I wandered through the streams where your stepmother was found and wondered what would have happened had you fallen into the water that day. How, compared to what the woman had endured, your tiny little body would have been beaten against rocks, pulled under the water over and over until you were lifeless, and still it would have battered you. I found your shoe one day, the one you'd lost."

He handed it to the man standing next to the podium and he brought it forward. When it was in her hand, she thought about how she'd tied it that morning and wondered if she'd get to run somewhere if there was time. She missed being outside.

"I thank you for this." He nodded and asked if he could finish now. "Of course. Please do."

"I know that you've been suffering. I've heard…there were all kinds of rumors about how you couldn't leave your home, how you'd been hidden away so that vultures would leave you alone. I just wanted to say…I needed to say that I'm sorry. I'm sorry that you had to go through this. No child should ever lose their parents like this, and none should have been treated like you were because of it. Instead of making you the bad guy, we should have tried to help you." He nodded to Hunter and the others. "You have a man there that loves you. I can see that, and I hope that you'll be able to move on with your life when this is over."

She answered more questions when he sat down. Slone asked Luke to keep an eye on the man. She wanted to find out as much about him as she could. Slone had a feeling he was more than just a reporter. Finally the question came that she'd been dreading.

"How did you get chewed up like you did? A doctor's report says that it was more than likely the branches around the water's edge. Others say you were mauled by an animal. You were never in the water, so that doesn't pan out; and then if you were mauled by an animal, why did he leave you there instead of taking you off to have you for lunch?"

"I'd like to ask you how you came to the conclusion that I was never in the water." He shrugged. "That's no answer. You said it as if you knew I wasn't. I'd just like to know how you know that."

"You were just on the edge of it, so that's how you got your shoe downstream. Or you could have just kicked it off and let it go. For all we know you could have body slammed your stepmother when she was trying to take you on a nice outing, and then cut yourself up so we'd all think you were the poor little girl."

"I see. And do you know a lot of six-year-olds that can body slam an adult? I don't. Perhaps you can show me just how that's even possible." She asked him to come forward. As he did, she stood as well. She slipped off her shoes and kicked them back to the table. Hunter stood up as if to come to her, and she shook her head. When Dave, the reporter, was in front of her, she stood about a foot away.

"Now what?" She threw her body at him, and he only took a step back. "You're trying to make a point. But I'm a little bigger than your stepmother was and considerably bigger than you."

"And that would be the point. I'm me back then, and you can be Eva." She slammed against him the second time, and he only backed up; this time, however, he also pushed her back. When she landed on her butt, she heard Hunter growl and they all turned to him. He looked...she wanted to say sexy, but it was more than that. Instead of getting up, she looked at the reporter. "You didn't just let me knock you around. Do you think that's what Eva would have done? And remember, I'm only six while you're an adult." She watched as he slid his sight to her. He was slightly thrown off by the growl, but he smiled down at her. Then he put out his hand and helped her to stand.

"Okay, you've made your point on this. But what about the wounds? How did you get those?"

"I don't know." He looked like he was going to say more, but she cut him off. "I was hurt and nearly drowned when they found me. After she ordered me to get into the water, I was shoved into it. I don't remember much other than having mouthfuls of water, and that if I didn't hang on I was dead. I didn't even know she had fallen in until I woke up in the hospital."

"Just how were you found?" Again she told him she didn't know. "You know, this only gives me more questions and not much in the way of answers. You should have a better story if you want the press to believe you."

"A better story or a better lie?" He didn't say anything to her question. "I suppose I could make up something. How about this? A large black wolf came from nowhere and hit his hind feet at Eva, knocking her way from me. As she went tumbling into the water, I was hanging onto the small weeds as hard as I could. I knew that all hope was lost and I was going to die. My daddy would miss me and I'd be dead. Then the wolf bit into my wrist. The pain was incredible and I screamed. Water filled my mouth again and choked. When I started to slip into the water again, he put his large paw onto my leg and tried to drag me out of the fast moving current. After that, I don't know what happened. Days later…no, weeks later, I woke in a hospital room to find out that not only had my stepmother died, but they had buried my daddy, too. You see, they found him in a freezer with a suicide note attached to his chest. It proclaimed that he could no longer live with my death. As he was dead before I was taken to the river, it's doubtful that he would have been able to write that, don't you think?"

"That's a good story but not possible." She only stared at him until he shrugged. "I guess you really don't know.

Not that it matters, I suppose. The only person who really knows what happened that day is you, and apparently you aren't talking."

"I'm talking, Dave, you're just not listening." He saluted her and turned to sit back down. She did as well. Slone answered questions for the next two hours, an hour longer than she'd said she would. As she moved out of the room, she was met by Hunter, who had gotten up just before the meeting was called to end. She sobbed in his arms, glad that it was over with, but knew that it was far from over.

"How about we go someplace." He lifted her chin when she didn't answer him. "I have a plan, Mrs. Emerson, and it requires you to be dressed properly and to take your hair down."

They were in the limo when she realized that she didn't have a clue where they were going. He told her to wait. She laid her head back on the seat thinking she'd like to ride her mate all the way to wherever it was they were going, and felt her body beginning to relax by degrees.

"I was going to jump on you." Yawning, she tried to work up the energy to follow through on what she'd said. "Just give me a minute here and I want to have you naked beneath me. I want to feel your cock inside of me."

He laughed a little, and she smiled. "You should know that where we're going has a nice bed and a hot tub. Have you ever had sex in a hot tub?"

"No." Another yawn. "Will it be fun?"

If he answered her, she didn't hear him. Suddenly her body simply shut down and she knew that whatever happened, he'd protect her because he loved her. And she loved him.

Chapter 13

Hunter watched her closely. Slone was having fun, but he knew what this was costing her. Every time a person came near her in the mammoth store, she would cringe a little and moved back. But in the hour they'd been there, she'd gotten better.

"I like this one. What do you think?" He eyed the bed and then cocked a brow at her. "You don't like it?"

There was laughter in her voice, and he decided he loved that sound. "If you plan for me to tie you to the canopy every night, then to the posts in the morning while I take you hard against it, then buy it. Otherwise, I think we should have something a little more…sturdy." She laughed and moved to the next display. Now, this one he liked.

The bed was a big four-poster kind that looked old even though he knew that it couldn't be. The bed itself looked like he could roll around in it for hours, and could see himself taking Slone on this one nightly. Pulling her to his body so that her bottom nestled tightly against his cock, he rocked into her and she moaned.

"I want to find a place right now and bend you over and take you hard." She nodded, and he nipped at her earlobe. "Where can we go?"

"You're serious?" He bit her again and then rocked into her holding onto her hips. "You're going to make me come like this. I have no idea where we can go."

Hunter took her hand and started walking. He knew that as badly as he wanted her right now, he'd come nearly as soon as he entered her. When he came to the restrooms he sent her in first, and then followed her when she told him it was clear. Going inside, he took her to the counter after locking the door, and took her mouth.

She'd worn another skirt today, and he loved it. Lifting her skirt up to her hips, he ripped her panties off. Her hands were busy at his pants when he lifted her blouse up with her bra and took her nipple into this mouth.

"I need to fuck you." She nodded and freed his cock. He let her fist him several times before he laid her back on the counter. "This is not going to be easy on you. I have had a powerful need to overpower you for hours."

"Take me." He moved between her opened thighs and entered her quickly. As soon as her ankles were around his hips, he moved in and out of her slowly while he nipped at her throat. "Hunter, don't play. Just fill me. I'm so close to coming now that I'm having a hard time holding back."

"Don't. Come for me." He lifted her up and took her against the wall. "Christ, do you have any idea how much I wish we were outside right now? I'd strip you down and have you running naked in the woods while I hunted you. Then I'd take you to the ground and eat your pussy until my beast was satisfied. Then I'd shift and fuck you."

She cried out and buried her face in his neck. He felt her teeth graze his throat, and he told her to bite. As soon as her teeth broke skin, Hunter took her shoulder and bit down hard as he came. Slone screamed her release again and again as she came with him.

The knocking on the door had him lifting his head. Turning, Hunter looked at her and smiled. "Do you think they heard us?"

"I'd be surprised if the store didn't hear us." She wrapped her arms around his shoulders, seeming to be in no hurry to get dressed. "When we get home, do you think you could do just what you said? I'd really like to see you in action."

"Taking you in the woods is going to be a good deal longer than this quickie." She nuzzled his neck again, and his cock jerked inside of her. But the person at the door knocked again, and he chuckled. "We need to get dressed and out of here before we're arrested."

As soon as he was dressed, he went to the door and opened it. The woman standing there looked at him for several seconds, then at the sign on the door. He grinned.

"Our honeymoon. We just can't keep our hands off each other." She nodded, and Slone came out fussing with her hair. He kissed her on the mouth and moved by the woman when he heard her sigh. He moved them toward the bedroom suite again. She flagged down a salesperson and they bought it in the largest size they had. Next was the living room.

They had several ideas in mind for this room. It would be the one they spent a lot of time in and they both wanted comfort over style. The salesperson in this department assured them they could have both. As he showed them two sets he liked, Slone looked at him and smiled.

"I want to have leather. Soft and buttery. Dark, too, with soft cotton pillows with chairs of the same material.

No coffee table but several end tables that would hold a cup of tea and nothing else. I want functional and practical. But above all else, I want comfort." He stared at her for several seconds, then nodded and asked them to follow him. As they entered the showroom, Hunter knew this was it. As soon as they moved into the room, he had his living room.

Slone seemed to think the same thing. As she made arrangements to have two couches and not any of the smaller love seats delivered to the house, as well as five big overstuffed chairs, Hunter's phone rang. He answered it wondering what his dad could want.

"Thought you'd like to know that the stuff you wanted from home arrived. I had a kick out of setting it up." Hunter smiled, thinking he hoped Slone liked it, too. "I'd completely forgotten that your mom kept everything you boys ever had. And I forgot how beautiful it was, too. Brought me to tears putting it together. And I had her old rocker sent up, too. Hope you don't mind."

"No. I think she'll love it. We looked at a couple here, but she didn't find anything she liked. She said it would tell her when she sat in it." His dad laughed. "Did the rest of the stuff come, too?"

"Yeah. They delivered it before the bed and things came. Did you know that with all this crate wood, I'm going to be able to build me a little green house?" He hoped his dad held off on that, too, as one of the crates held the makings for a large greenhouse that Slone had ordered for the house. "I checked the mail, too, and there my catalog was. Slone and I are going to have a good old time come spring. I have an idea we should expand our gardens."

"Dad, she'll be huge with my child by the time gardening comes around. Don't you think you should wait until next year?" He laughed, and Hunter did, too. He turned to look at her as she studied lamps. "Christ, Dad. I had no idea that falling in love could be so wonderfully exhausting."

He flushed when his dad laughed. It wasn't what he'd meant, but there was no telling his dad that. When he finally stopped laughing, Hunter smiled at him. His dad was having a grand time as well.

"I spoke to Luke about an hour ago. He said the Feds were there going through all the computers and files. The boy, Allen, he's beside himself with worry that he might be in trouble. I don't think that kid has a thing to worry about. Did you know he had a record?" Hunter told him that he didn't. "Seems he got himself in trouble a few years back and he lost his ability to drive and own a car. I didn't know they were so hard on people when they were caught on expired licenses. He has to go for seven years without it. Kid's been riding his bike all over town, even in winter. Luke told me he was going to have a taxi pick him up when the weather was poor."

"It doesn't bother Luke that he has a record, I'm assuming." Dad said it didn't seem to and told him that Luke thought it was funny that he'd never told Conklin but had told him the first day. "He'll be a big help to Luke once they get things going."

"I agree. And so you know, Jarrett is looking at that building on Tenth. He seems to think he can make it work. Hell, I thought maybe he'd make it work even if he had to work in a shed. Never seen him so excited before. None of you boys, I guess." His dad cleared his throat before he continued. "How is darlin' doing? She's not over doing it, is she?"

"No. She's doing just fine. Arguing with a salesperson right now. I think she wants it brought today and they're telling her later. She never was one to wait once she got something in her head." His dad cackled laughing. "Dad, are you happy with us? This morning, before we left...well, she was worried that you'd changed your mind."

"No, not changed my mind. I'm a little overwhelmed by this all, if you want to know the truth. Never thought we'd be living in this kind of luxury before, much less me having a grandbaby, too. I thought you boys would be as old as me before a woman came along to take you. You have no idea how happy I am that at least one of you have gotten up off your asses and started moving in the general direction of making me a granddad."

"I'm hoping we make you a granddad a few times before you start shoving up daisies. Slone said that now that she can have them, she never wants to quit." Hunter watched her for a few seconds more before he continued. "Dad, I love you."

"And I love you, too, son. You enjoy your day shopping with her. I got things under control here. And when she gets here, the baby's room will blow her away."

He knew it would, too.

As they walked around the kitchen looking at things he had no idea about, he thought about how lucky he was. A woman who loved him, a baby on the way, and more in the way of money than he'd ever had in his entire life. He wandered over to one of the appliances that he had no idea what it was and leaned against the counter. Hunter laughed when Slone asked for the man in the living room section to come and help her.

"No. If he doesn't help me, I will go to a store that needs my money more than you do. I've spent a great deal of money already and while I hate to be a pain in the ass, if he can't help me, then...well, I'll find someone who can." The woman stuttered at her for several seconds, and Slone turned and walked away. Before she got to Hunter, the store manager caught up with her and had the young man with him to assist.

"He'll be at your beck and call for the duration of your time here. And if you need to come back, I'll make sure that he's here as well." Slone nodded and winked at him. He loved it when she got all bossy with people. As the young man, Tim Leader, helped her out, Hunter sat at the kitchen table closest to him. He didn't know shit about a kitchen and since Slone had a list from Lee, he knew that she'd make short work of this part of the shopping, too. He called Pete.

"I have the meeting set up for Friday night. And I've made sure that everyone knows to keep it kind of on the down low. They'll approach her in small groups so as not to overwhelm her. And the women have already started cooking. I'm guessing there will be leftovers for a year from this thing." Hunter doubted that and said as much. "Yeah, here's a bachelor hoping there are a few anyway."

The pack was going to meet him and his family as well as their new she-alpha. A few of them had already spoken to him as well as Slone, but a lot of them had not. After the conference the other day, more and more times than not, Slone could be found in the town talking to someone about one thing or another. He knew that it scared her a great deal, but she was working through it most of the time.

When she sat down at the table with him, he took her hand.

"Tim is going to help me get the rest of the bedroom furniture picked out. Do you want to go and meet Graham now? He said it wasn't important, but he wanted to talk to you." Hunter kissed her hand and stood up. "And then we'll have dinner and go home, right?"

"I thought we'd stay here for the night. Rent a room and have some super sex on a big bed. Yours is a little on the small size when it comes to the kind of making love I have in mind." She tensed up for a second, then nodded. "You're the love of my life. So if you want to go home, we will."

"I want to stay. I do. If you want to find us a place, then I can meet you there later. This place has an amazing lingerie section and I thought I'd go and see what I can find for you."

He growled low and pulled her to him for a kiss. Before he got them both into trouble, he walked away. Her giggling made him smile and he could not wait until tonight. He called Graham to let him know he was on his way. It was going to be a long day waiting for night to come, Hunter just knew it.

~~~

She wondered what she was doing there and took several deep breaths before she could take another step. Slone knew that sending Hunter away was a big step in the right direction, but now she was alone in a store with hundreds of people. Slone knew that she was going to faint and looked around for a place to hide. Then Tim was in front of her.

"Take a deep breath and let it out slowly." She shook her head, and he nodded. "You can do it. Just let it out

slowly by counting to ten. I'll count with you. One. Two...
come on, Mrs. Emerson, you can do this."

"I'm going to pass out." He shook his head and smiled
at her. "You have no idea how terrified I am. I should...I
need my husband."

"I do know how terrified you are. Take a deep breath
again and let it out. Not too fast or you're going to pass out
and show the world that you fell on your face in the mall.
There are people with cell phones just waiting for
something like this to happen so they can post it on their
websites. They don't care who you are or what you might
be suffering, they just do it. Come on now, you're doing
much better."

"How do you know?" Tim shrugged. "You were hurt
like this, right? Someone...you have panic attacks, too?
How can you do this?"

"Not me. My mom. We would go to the store and I'd
have to talk her down like this. She never lost it often, but
she did on occasion. It was something she had no control
over when it hit. You're doing much better." She nodded
as she started to feel less closed in. "A woman recorded her
while she was sobbing in the ladies' room. Then she posted
it to one of those sites. Mom never left the house again
until she died."

"I'm so sorry." Tim shrugged, but she could see that it
hurt him. When he let go of her hands, she took one back
and squeezed it tightly into her own. "You saved me. I
don't mean just from an embarrassment. But you actually
saved me from running out of here and into the street. I
don't care for people on my best day. I should have known
better than to do this right now."

He moved with her toward the bedroom section again.
When he turned to her, she knew that whatever it was he

wanted was going to be his. He looked around before speaking in low tones.

"I know who you are." She felt the hair on her arms dance, and she looked around, too. "I haven't said anything to anyone here, but I knew the moment you came in. You were in the paper a few weeks back when you got the mayor in your town fired."

"I didn't fire him. He did that all on his own." He nodded and grinned. "You have been helping me because of that?"

"Oh no." He looked shocked, and she felt horrible for saying it to him. "Oh no. I just liked the way you knew what you wanted and wasn't going to take no for an answer. It's why I went to get the store manager. I knew that he'd want you happy. I never told him who you were, just that you'd spent a great deal of money and it looked like you might be canceling it because of something that was said to you. I appreciate you asking me to help you." She nodded.

As she picked out five-bedroom suites to fill the other rooms, she wondered if he would work out as her assistant. Luke and Hunter both told her to find someone to help her with the daily paperwork that was going to come her way, and she thought he'd work out well.

"Do you like selling furniture to picky women?" He laughed as he helped her pick out a bedroom set for Cash. It was firm and solid like the man. "I mean, is this what you want to do?"

"No. I don't know anyone who would want to work in customer service. It's okay for some, but not for me. I do it because it pays the bills." She nodded. "Do you know of a job opening somewhere else? It would have to pay well. I make commissions here. They aren't great, not like today's will be, but they help with the bills. I'm living in my mom's house, and it needs some work done to it."

"I might be able to help you with that as well. I need an assistant. It does involve some customer service work, and you'd—"

"I'll take it." She laughed, and he did as well. "I'm serious. Whatever it is, I'll work with you. I need to get something better and if you're serious, I'm willing to do it."

She told him about the background checks and other things she'd have to run, and he assured her that it wouldn't be an issue. When she finished with her purchases, she gave him her name and number and called Luke. He said he'd take care of it right away and spoke to Tim. After they hung up, she was glad now that Hunter had left her and she'd met this young man. They were going to work well together.

Slone and Tim finished up in no time. As she made arrangements to have things delivered to her house, she wondered if any of the men in her life would like what she'd gotten them. Especially Hunter. The nightie that she got him was almost embarrassing to her. She could not wait to see his face when she showed it to him. Smiling, she left the store and headed to the hotel he'd made arrangements for them to stay in. It was going to be a very fun night. She got into the tub as soon as she arrived and used some of the wonderful smelling lotions she'd gotten as well.

As soon as she heard the key slide in the lock, she held her breath. He'd told her that he was on his way up to change and that they were having dinner with Luke in an hour. Slone wondered if that was going to be enough time for what she had in mind for Hunter, but didn't really care. She was lying on the bed when he came into the room.

He stood in the doorway staring at her for so long she wondered if he was upset. When he took off his jacket and tossed it in the general direction of the chair, she watched him move across the room toward her as he undressed.

"You bought this today?" She nodded and ran her fingers over the small squares of silk that just barely covered her breasts. "I hope you didn't pay too much for it because it's going to be nothing but rags when I'm finished with you."

"You aren't going to get to take it off me. I'm going to take it off me for you." He nodded and licked his lips as he stood within touching distance of her. "I'm going to strip you down as well. How would you like that?"

"Slow and easy." She stood up, and he moaned. "Do you have any idea how sexy you look right now? Turn for me. Slowly."

She turned slowly and then looked at him over her shoulder. She liked the way he was staring at her, and she winked at him as she turned and moved behind him.

"I'm going to strip you down. Then I'm going to taste all of you. Starting with your cock." He groaned, and she rubbed her hand over his thick cock. "Maybe we won't get much further than that, as hard as you are."

"Are you going to take me into your mouth, Slone?" She nodded and dropped to her knees in front of him. "Then we won't get much further than that. Because the moment I slide down the back of your throat, I'm going to come. The thought of you…Christ, you look good enough to eat right now."

"I love it when you eat me. I come so hard just knowing that you're drinking my juices." She squealed when she was suddenly airborne. He had picked her up and tossed her on the bed so fast that she bounced twice before she landed in the middle. He was on her before she could guess what he was going to do.

"I told you I was close." His hands slid up her thighs and under the tiny little strings at the sides of her panties. "You're going to have to suck me some other time. Right now I need to lap at your pussy until you come down my throat. Then I'm going to fuck you from behind until you scream out my name."

He didn't waste any time as he buried his face between her legs. She screamed when he nipped at her clit and came hard and fast. He was lapping at her before she could catch her breath, and came twice more before he lifted his head and looked at her.

"I want to fuck you like this." She nodded as he moved up her body, putting her legs on his shoulders. "It's going to be deep and hard. I want you to come as many times as you can as you take me."

He entered her just as her hips came up off the bed. He had her nearly bent in half when he started pounding into her. She had never had him this deep before. And when he tore off her nightie, she reached up and took her nipples in her fingers and twisted them hard. Her climax took her so hard she nearly fainted from it. When he pulled his cock from her, she reached for him, but he pushed her away.

"On your knees. I need to pound into you like an animal." She moved to do his bidding but wasn't fast enough. He flipped her over and jerked her to his cock so fast that she cried out again.

He curled his body around her and fucked her in fast, hard strokes until she was dizzy from it. As soon as he cupped her breast, he licked along her shoulder, and she knew that he was going to bite her. She pressed back against him as she prepared her for his marking.

"While you come, I'm going to bite you. Hard. And when I do, I'm going to hurt you. The need to claim you is making my wolf crazy." She felt his teeth graze her shoulder. "Christ, I need you."

She screamed loud and long when he bit her. Slone felt her shoulder crush under his bite and knew that his wolf was just as much a part of him as Hunter was. When he pulled back, scarring her back with his teeth, Slone felt claws dig deep into her hips and felt her own wolf snarl at her to let go when he did. As soon as Hunter threw back his head and howled, his voice echoing around the room, Slone did as well. Her entire body was alive with the climax that ripped from her. As she lay under him, breathing hard and feeling fucking fantastic, she wondered if it would always be like this for them. Hunter chuckled and sealed the wound at her shoulder.

"You will always be my mate and I will forever want to mark you. So in answer to your thoughts, yes, it will always be like this between us."

"I'm glad. I don't know what I'd do without you." He told her he didn't want to find out what life would be without her and pulled her into his arms when he lay on the bed. "We're going to be late."

Laughing, she told him she didn't care and closed her eyes. "Luke will have to find his own mate and he'll understand." And she hoped that they all found their mates so they could all feel this wonderful all the time.

About the Author

Kathi Barton, author of the bestselling series Force of Nature, lives in Nashport, Ohio with her husband Paul. In addition to writing full time Kathi likes to spend time with her eight grandkids, three children and three children-in-laws. She writes to relax and have fun.

Her muse, a cross between Jimmy Stewart and Hugh Jackman brings them to life for her readers in a way that has them coming back time and again for more. Her favorite genre is paranormal romance with a great deal of spice. You can visit Kathi on line and drop her an email if you'd like. She loves hearing from her fans. aaronskiss@gmail.com.

Follow Kathi on her blog:
http://kathisbartonauthor.blogspot.com/

.

* 9 7 8 1 6 2 9 8 9 1 2 8 6 *